"Marilyn Baxter's engaging and thoroughly modern twist on a marriage of convenience will have you laughing, crying, cheering and sighing! A perfect romance!"

—*New York Times* Bestselling Author Roxanne St. Claire

SHOOTING FOR THE STARS

When it comes to relationships, Tess Callahan is gun-shy. An ambitious Atlanta divorce attorney, she's seen the aftermath of relationships gone bad, which is why she has no time in her life for any man except for Nick Russo. Handsome and exciting, he's the perfect choice to give her all she desires—including the fact he's never around long enough for things to get complicated. Until suddenly they do.

Nick Russo has the world. His job as a photographer takes him everywhere, and he wouldn't give that life up for anyone, not even the beautiful and brilliant Tess Callahan. Or so he thinks. An unexpected pregnancy is about to bring everything into focus, a brighter and more colorful world than he ever thought to imagine. The possibilities are endless, and they're something he can capture not just on film but in reality.

PICTURE THIS

Marilyn Baxter

www.BOROUGHSPUBLISHINGGROUP.com

PICTURE THIS
Copyright © 2015 Marilyn Puett

ISBN 978-1942886-58-7

To Rhonda Nelson. If you look up the term "steel magnolia" in the dictionary, it will be illustrated with her picture. Rhonda is a busy writer with a family and a successful career, but she took time to have dinner with a struggling writer (AKA moi) and helped me get this book on the right track. If you've never read one of Rhonda's books, I encourage you to do so. They are filled with hot, sexy heroes, smart, sassy heroines, and Rhonda's trademark humor. Thank you, Rhonda, for your guidance and advice, otherwise Tess and Nick would still be floundering in chapter one.

ACKNOWLEDGMENTS

To Michelle Klayman, the fearless leader of Boroughs Publishing Group, for adding even more to your already full plate when duty called. Thank you for your guidance and understanding. Shall we form our own chapter of the Cary Grant fan club?

And to Karen, Paula and Deb, for whom the labor and delivery nurses in this book were named. Six years ago you were strangers to me, then circumstances brought us all together. In a different sense, you were *my* nurses. You nursed my soul when I was despondent. You gave me hope and encouragement to keep on keeping on. And now you add beauty, wisdom, laughter, and best of all, tons and tons of fun, to the new life you helped me build. Thank you for being my dearest friends. You are the sisters of my heart.

CONTENTS

PICTURE THIS

Chapter One

"Sometimes I don't know if you're coming or going."

Tess Callahan leaned back against the pillow and watched as Nick Russo, her best friend with benefits—her *only* friend with benefits, which included strong arms, a broad, solid chest and a fine ass she could admire forever—jotted flight information on a scrap of paper he'd torn from one of her magazines. He could have torn a whole page out and it wouldn't have mattered; she never had the time to read them anyway.

Her nightstand drawer held only breath mints, lip balm, an assortment of condoms and lubricants and a comic book version of the Kama Sutra—a gag gift from an office Christmas party. Unlike her office in downtown Atlanta, which was organized down to the length of the pencils in the holder on her desk, she preferred her home life to be more casual and less rigid.

"Where to this time?" she asked.

Nick turned off his cell phone, shoved it and the scrap of paper into the pocket of the jeans he'd flung across the back of a chair in the corner and slid back under the covers.

"Australia," he replied with a heavy sigh. "Again. And…I think it's been pretty obvious tonight that I've been coming and coming." Nick peered from beneath dark eyebrows, which slashed across his forehead and sent her a look that could have melted steel. He added a wink. "And coming. And from the sound of things, I believe I've satisfied you."

A shiver danced down Tess's spine from the sensuality that oozed from every pore in Nick's body.

Tall and lean, with dark hair and eyes that reflected his Italian heritage, the man's looks alone could charm the panties off a woman. Add in a killer body, a wicked sense of humor and above-average intelligence, Nick was any woman's idea of a fine catch—if she was looking for a husband.

And Tess was not.

She scooted next to all six feet, two inches of him. He was hot—literally. He emitted heat like a blast furnace, and right now Tess needed heat. She had cooled off when Nick had left the bed to check the call that had come in somewhere between orgasms two and three—or was it three and four? She had lost count. Now she wanted more. More warmth and more of Nick, especially since, from his side of the phone conversation, he would be leaving again soon.

He worked as a photographer for a highly respected magazine. The job required extensive worldwide travel, often landing him in perilous war zones or in the middle of natural disasters. Thank goodness Tess had no romantic designs on Nick. She wasn't sure she could take losing another man in her life.

"Come here," he whispered, his voice raspy with obvious desire. He pulled her body against his in the spooning position they both enjoyed. His arms engulfed her and she soaked up his body heat, wiggling back further, pressing her butt into his groin. Instantly she felt his body react and he exhaled a deep groan.

"You are insatiable," he said, inching his hand down her abdomen. "Beyond insatiable. And I have to go home and pack for a flight at noon tomorrow."

"Then we'd better hurry, huh?"

Nick reached between her thighs and brushed his fingertips against her dampness. She responded with an appreciative moan of approval and pushed her body toward his hand. He pressed two fingers against her and began a steady, rhythmic massage. Already hypersensitive from their previous coupling, Tess responded quickly and within minutes a firestorm burst in her veins.

Before her heart rate had even begun to decelerate, Nick had pulled a foil pack from beneath the pillow and sheathed himself. He moved into position over her and paused for a moment, his gaze locked with hers. She shifted her legs to open herself to him and held out her arms in encouragement.

Nick wasted no time accepting her invitation. He pressed the tip of his erection to her core and pushed inside slowly. Tess wrapped her legs around him, drawing him closer. Urging him deeper.

"Faster," she begged, breathless with pleasure.

"This is the third time tonight, and I don't want to hurt you," he said, sliding a bit deeper.

Tess tightened her feminine muscles around him, encouraging him. "You're not hurting me. And it's the fourth time, but who's counting?"

Nick's laugh morphed into a groan as she arched upward and took him fully inside. She closed her eyes and concentrated on the sensations assaulting every one of her senses—the feel of him inside her, the musky smell of their sex coating him, the quiver of his biceps as they supported his weight, the sound of his breath catching in his throat.

"Make me come again before you go." She uttered the words more as a command than a request, but Nick responded without argument.

He withdrew, and then plunged back into her, setting a pace that soon caused both of them to be covered in a fine sheen of perspiration, each gasping for the next breath almost in unison.

"I'm almost…"

Nick groaned just as Tess arched again, her breath catching in her throat as stars burst behind her closed lids.

"Look at me," Nick commanded. "I want to see your eyes."

She focused her gaze intently on his as he gave a final thrust, groaned and collapsed against her. He rolled them both over, taking his weight from her, and he pressed a gentle kiss to her neck.

"That," he whispered next to her ear, "was amazing. Damn, woman. You're going to kill me one of these days."

"Mmmmm. *You* are amazing. And why would I kill such a remarkable lover?" Tess let her hands roam his strong chest and biceps as if memorizing his body until their next night together, whenever that might be.

She had no complaints though. While his job kept him out of town, and often out of the country, for long stretches, when he was in Atlanta he was more than accommodating in meeting her sexual needs. And she was always more than happy to reciprocate.

They had met two years before at a Halloween party where he had worn a Prince Charming costume—and worn it as if he were a prince in real life—and she had been dressed as Marilyn Monroe in *The Seven Year Itch*. At midnight, instead of losing a glass slipper so Prince Charming would search to find her, they had dashed to her apartment; both lost their costumes and consummated their new relationship. Tess had never believed in love at first sight, and this wasn't love. It was pure lust, and the arrangement seemed to work for them both.

Tess had continued to date other men for a while, but none compared to her personal prince. A little remarkable sex was better than a lot of mediocre or even lousy sex. So now she accepted to wait until Nick could be the one providing her with sexual satisfaction.

She snuggled closer then shifted back into their familiar spooning position.

"Get some sleep," Nick crooned. "I have to leave in a couple hours, but you don't have to get up with me."

She knew she'd wake anyway when his warmth disappeared from the bed. She would shower with him, maybe try for round number five and then wave good-bye from the front door.

Nick was just good-time sex. Great-time sex. Best-ever sex. No strings, no commitments, no problems. And definitely no emotions.

That lie sat like a stone in the pit of her stomach. A tiny piece of her heart was starting to really enjoy his company and wonder what—or who—he was doing when he wasn't with her. His job took him to numerous places. Was there a woman in each of them? Or more than one?

She would simply have to put out that tiny fire of emotion. She hadn't worked hard to build a successful career as an attorney for nothing. No man would ever leave her like her mother had been left.

Not even best-ever sex partner Nick Russo.

*****

Nick woke before dawn, his brain already calculating what he'd need for this trip to Australia. It would be his third trip down under since going to work for *Earth Events* magazine five years earlier.

He had spent three weeks in January in the bush photographing a piece about Aboriginal bush tucker and the first week of February off the clock in Sydney shooting the Eveleigh Market, taking photos of the various vendors and artisans and their wares. If the photos turned out as he hoped, he would frame them and sell them on consignment at a friend's gallery. The remainder of the month found him hopping all over Europe. The first of March he had covered an attempted military coup in some godforsaken area of West Africa and finally he'd landed back in Atlanta in the middle of the month.

After he'd spent a respectable amount of time with his parents, he had cashed in on some overdue benefits from Tess.

He enjoyed the unpredictable nature of his work and rarely said no to any assignment that came his way. Nick had made a name for himself as both a proficient and reliable photographer. But even a travel junkie like him needed the occasional break, and he had thought of nothing but Tess for the entire flight back from Africa.

Too bad that archaeology team had made a significant discovery of rock art in the outback or he would still be coming instead of going halfway around the world again. The thought of spending over a day either on a plane or in an airport terminal grated at his nerves, and just for a moment—that one sweet moment when Tess had come apart in his arms again and he had followed her over the edge—he had considered saying no to leaving.

Nick had spent far too many years building up his reputation as the man most willing to go the extra mile for the perfect picture. No way would he let some upstart get a crack at what could be a career-defining photo. Not a chance.

He showered and dressed quickly in well-worn jeans and a fleece pullover, pulled on his socks, then shoved his feet into a pair of boots before glancing around to make sure he had gathered all his belongings. He traveled light, but everything he had was essential.

With any luck he'd be back home in a few weeks to take the long-overdue vacation his boss had promised way too many months ago. He knew exactly where he planned to spend it—and with whom.

April in Atlanta could be cool, so he had investigated renting a seaside villa in Curaçao. He and Tess could snorkel in the warm equatorial waters by day, dine on fresh seafood in Willemstad by night, take a moonlight swim in the villa's secluded pool after dinner and then escape to the canopied bed in the master suite—if they even managed to make it to the bedroom.

Unlike most of the women he had dated in the past, Tess was the perfect woman for him: smart, beautiful, but not self-absorbed; plus she was independent and a firecracker in bed. She expected nothing except companionship, good conversation and great sex, which he made every effort to deliver along with the occasional gourmet dinner. The woman had a thing for lobster and Nick admitted to himself he was more than glad to pay the market price for those ridiculously oversized crawdads in order to keep her happy.

Nick winced at the thought. That made their relationship sound mercenary, and Tess Callahan was most definitely not a woman for sale. They also didn't have a *relationship*, just an exceptional mutually satisfying arrangement. But the sex *was* great.

He made his way to the side of the bed and contemplated waking her to say good-bye. She shifted in her sleep and the movement caused the sheet to drop, exposing her bare breasts and making him wish he could tell his editor he didn't want to follow the yellow brick road to Oz.

She shivered against the early morning chill and Nick watched as her nipples puckered from the cold. He grasped the edge of the floral sheet and covered her, not only to warm her but to calm his body as it reacted to the sight of her naked one. He tucked the soft material around her then leaned over to press his lips gently to her forehead.

He scribbled a note and propped it on the desk in her living room.

Didn't want to disturb your beauty sleep. Call you when I get back and we'll get out of town to someplace warm. ~Nick.

He left the apartment, made sure the door was locked behind him and returned to his mental packing list. He dreaded the twenty-seven-hour trip ahead of him. The only good part about this assignment was knowing that Tess would be there when he returned.

Chapter Two

<u>Seven months later</u>

Tess stared at the wall display containing various types and sizes of screwdrivers and muttered a curse. She could screw an adulterous husband to the wall in court, and did so with great pleasure on a regular basis as a top-notch divorce attorney with Atlanta's premier law firm, Hightower, Leggett and Beck. So why couldn't she just as skillfully navigate this maze of tools and figure out which one she needed?

Obviously, furniture assembly was another matter, and when she'd rushed to Do-It-Yourself Depot to buy hand tools for her latest project, she had not realized she would have such a sizeable variety from which to choose.

Nick would have known without hesitation. She had accompanied him to this store on many occasions to buy supplies for his furniture-refinishing hobby. She had even paused in the cabinet section and considered buying new knobs for the chest she needed to assemble. Being in this store brought back memories, and she glanced right and then left, wondering if maybe he was shopping there today as he did on many Saturdays.

She shook off the thought because odds were he wasn't even in town.

"Can I help you, ma'am?" A tall, sandy-haired boy who didn't look old enough to be out of high school, much less know anything about hand tools, rocked back on his heels and adjusted the nametag that read "Rick."

"I'm putting together a chest of drawers and need a screwdriver." She glanced at her list, which contained several other small tools she needed as well.

"What kind?" the boy asked. "Slotted? Phillips head? What about a socket screwdriver? Is it a square or star drive? Or sometimes furniture requires an Allen wrench. Did you check to see if it came with an Allen wrench?"

Tess stifled another curse along with the urge to pummel the boy with the claw hammer in her left hand. This was definitely not her favorite way to spend a Saturday morning.

"The directions specifically said screwdriver, so I'm going to operate on the presumption that no wrench is needed nor was one provided."

"But you don't know if you need a slotted or Phillips, do you? And what about the size?" He moved to the display, removed a red-handled tool and balanced it in his palm. "You have your blade length and then the driver head width to consider with a slotted one, whereas your Phillips head comes in numbered sizes that correspond to various screw sizes."

Tess's head swam with the overload of unsolicited screwdriver information delivered by the young store clerk. She closed her eyes and squeezed the bridge of her nose between two fingers in an attempt to fend off an impending headache.

"Or maybe you'd like one of these cordless screwdriver sets," Rick suggested, moving a few feet further down the aisle and pulling a box off the shelf. "This one is variable speed and has a hex-type chuck. Of course you'll need to buy the accessory set of bits and those will pretty much cover most any slotted or Phillips head screws you'd ever come in contact with. And this one is free with a two-hundred-and-fifty-dollar purchase."

"Maybe I should just go home and check the directions and make sure of what I need." Tess needed a cordless screwdriver set like she needed a third thumb. Maybe she could just use the end of a kitchen knife and accomplish her task.

"Or you could just ask your husband. Heck, he probably has whatever you need out in the garage anyway. But if he doesn't you tell him to come see Rick and I'll fix him up with whatever the little woman needs to put together that chest."

Tess tightened her grip on the hammer and revisited her earlier thoughts about using it. She knew she would be committing a felony. At the moment, though, she wasn't sure she cared. Calling the manager and pointing out that Rick was a prime candidate for demonstrating how to drive away customers in one easy step was beginning to look like a reasonable alternative. If she didn't use the hammer first.

Exhaling slowly, she chose her words carefully and said through gritted teeth, "I don't have a husband, Rick, and this *little woman* resents your insinuation that she can't buy a screwdriver by herself or that she needs a man to help assemble a piece of furniture. I'll just come back when I've read the directions and know for sure what I need." She mentally castigated herself for being so ill-prepared. On the job, she prided herself on solid and thorough preparation for every case she handled.

Must be the hormones, she thought.

"Should you even be assembling furniture in…you know…your condition?" Rick blushed as if embarrassed by the mention of pregnancy.

The headache was full-blown now, a brutal throb behind one eye, and she could feel the infusion of acid to her stomach as her anger level increased.

"Probably not, because women in…you know…*my condition* are weak, helpless little creatures who can't even think for themselves much less put together a piece of furniture. But since I don't have a husband—because it *is* possible to have a baby all on your own these days—I'll just have to figure this out all by my weak, helpless little self. And once I do, Rick, I won't ever be coming back here to shop since your employer obviously hasn't sent his employees through sensitivity training and I certainly don't like being insulted when I'm spending my hard-earned money." Her voice rose in tone and anger with each sentence.

"But what about your hammer?" he asked as she turned to walk away.

Tess slammed the tool down on an adjacent counter with all the strength her anger and headache had given her. The noise echoed through the open building like a gunshot and knocked over several display stands of small items.

"What about it, Rick?" she yelled in a challenge.

The young man swallowed and grabbed the hammer with one swift move. "I'll just put this away for you, ma'am. You have a nice day now and thank you so much for shopping at…" His words trailed off and he beat a hasty retreat as Tess skewered him with a disdainful look that could best be described as a death stare.

She stomped through the store, madder than an angry hornet and vowed never to set foot in Do-It-Yourself Depot again. Why did they have to put the hand tools section so far from the front door anyway? As she wove her way around other customers, she mentally composed a scathing letter to their CEO, castigating him and his entire operation for hiring employees with misogynistic attitudes and automatic assumptions that pregnant women should have husbands and were too helpless to do things for themselves. She would make damn sure the words "complete failure to pass sensitivity training" would be front and center in her letter.

She had managed quite nicely for the past seven months, and she would continue to manage for the remaining eight weeks of her pregnancy. Of course, she hadn't needed a screwdriver up until this point. Would raising a child be this complicated?

When she reached the paint department, she felt the baby shift and kick as if in response to the clerk's patronizing and sexist attitude. She had dealt with men like him throughout her career in family law, and she achieved enormous satisfaction from slicing them off at the knees in court.

Her own childhood had been marred and scarred by her father's misdeeds. With the help of the other attorneys in the firm where she was employed, they made sure cheating husbands paid the price instead of letting their innocent wives and children bear the brunt of the emotional and financial consequences of divorce.

Tess shuffled past the paint sample cards and continued toward the exit. As she reached a display of light fixtures directly in front of the main exit, the muscles in her belly contracted. She paused, grabbed the edge of the display shelving and breathed through it. She'd been having Braxton Hicks contractions for weeks, but this one was especially strong.

"Calm down, sweetie. I'm not quite ready for you yet, and thank to Rick the Prick, it's going to take a little longer." She patted her belly as she spoke to her unborn child, not caring if anyone overheard—not even Rick himself.

As the automatic doors whisked open, a breeze swept across her and cooled her overheated face. It also blew her shopping list out of her hand and whipped it down the aisle behind her.

"Oh, hell." Huffing out an exasperated breath, Tess absentmindedly rubbed her lower back, turned to chase down her list and found herself face to face with Nick Russo.

*****

Lately, every woman with short, spiky dark brown hair had begun to resemble Tess, including the waddling pregnant one he had spotted with a hammer in one hand at Do-It-Yourself Depot. Pregnancy aside, it couldn't be Tess. She didn't shop for paint and tools and plumbing supplies. Tess shopped at major department stores and trendy boutiques and had a landlord who would handle repairs to her apartment. The same apartment where he had spent many nights up until the previous spring when he'd made a serious decision about the two of them—a decision he had questioned often.

Nick had found the stain and varnish he needed for his current refinishing project, which was a rough-hewn antique sideboard he planned to give his sister Bella and her fiancé as a gift for their as-yet-unscheduled wedding. Then he had selected drawer pulls and was heading toward the self-service check-out when he saw the pregnant woman again. This time she was leaning against a display shelf and was massaging her back, which undoubtedly hurt given the advanced stage of her pregnancy. He had learned enough about pregnant women from his other sister Angie to know they suffered from backaches and wild mood swings.

He couldn't imagine Tess pregnant any more than he could imagine her shopping here. She was married to her job and he was married to his, much to his mother's utter disappointment. At least once a week she called, texted or emailed and somehow hinted that she wished he would find himself a nice girl, marry, settle down and give her more grandchildren.

He was pulled from his woolgathering when he saw a piece of paper, which had blown from the woman's hand and was skittering toward him along the concrete floor. He hurried to retrieve it for her. The woman looked ready to deliver and he was sure she couldn't touch her knees, much less pick anything up off the floor. Carol Russo might have a son who was allergic to marriage, but she had raised a gentleman.

Nick shifted his shopping basket to his left hand, scooped up the paper with the other and rose to face the woman. "Here you go, ma—," he began. He froze then stumbled backward a few steps as he stared into Tess Callahan's green eyes.

"Tess," he began, scrambling for something—*anything*—to say to her and trying not to stare at her abdomen, which was prominent beneath the form-fitting top she wore. His mind raced as he counted back the months since he had left for Australia. Then, like an idiot, he said the first thing that came to mind. "How've you been?"

Good going, Russo. How the hell do you think she's been?

Tess glanced downward at her protruding abdomen, then leveled her gaze at him. "I'll give you three guesses, and the first two don't count." Her tone dripped with sarcasm. "Much as I'd love to stay and chat with you, I really need to get home, have a meltdown and assemble a chest of drawers."

"Assemble a chest of drawers? You?" Nick bit the inside of his cheek to stifle a laugh then remembered how he had seen her rubbing her back earlier. "Should you be doing that in your…uhm…condition?" He waved his hand vaguely in the direction of her belly. "Aren't you supposed to take it easy? You know, no hot tubs, no standing for long periods, no heavy lifting, no attempted furniture assembly?"

"And you're an expert on pregnancy from which medical school?" She cocked her head to one side and raised an eyebrow.

Nick was no expert on pregnancy, but the strong possibility that Tess was pregnant with his child kept edging its way into his thoughts.

"Give me that." Tess snatched the piece of paper from his hand and ripped it in the process. "Dammit, I am not an invalid. I'm just pregnant. And I can do whatever I damn well please." Her voice climbed an octave on the last word.

"I didn't, I wasn't—"

"Yes you damn sure were. You and that asshole Rick in hardware and everybody else have been trying to run my life and tell me what I can and cannot do."

Nick opened his mouth to remind her he had been gone for the last seven months and couldn't possibly have tried to run her life. He thought better of it and let her continue with her rant.

"I can run my own life and assemble whatever I want. I'm perfectly capable of taking care of—"

Tess stopped mid-sentence and bit back a groan. Her arm cradled her belly and she drew in a sharp breath of air before doubling over and crying out in pain.

Nick rushed to her side and steadied her. "Tell me what I can do to help. Do you need me to call anyone?" he asked.

Tess shook her head. "No. It's okay. I just need to sit down for a few minutes and I'll be fine."

Nick led her to a stack of pallets and helped her get situated. "You don't look fine to me, Tess. You look awfully pale. Are you sure you don't want me to do something?"

She glared at him. "Like boil water? No, really, I'm—" She cried out again, this time wrapping both arms around her middle.

Nick watched a tear escape from one eye and track down her cheek. Tess never cried. Never. Then she moaned as another wave of pain overtook her, and she squeezed Nick's hand like a vise.

"Are you in labor, Tessie?" he asked, reverting to his pet name for her. Now wasn't the time to ask the dozens of questions he had about her being pregnant. She was obviously in distress. Should he offer to drive her home? To the hospital? Call 911 and let them handle it since his experience with labor was several degrees removed from firsthand? Given the size of her belly, could her baby be on the way? He mentally castigated himself for not paying more attention when his sister and sister-in-law were pregnant.

She shook her head as she took long, deep breaths then relaxed against him. He wiped away the tear and let the pad of his thumb linger at her jawline.

"I'm okay. I had to run errands today and I probably just overdid it. I need to go home and—"

"Put together a piece of furniture? Won't that be overdoing it a bit too?" he asked, his concern for her genuine.

"Go to hell, Nick." Tess pushed against the pallet and stood, wobbling a bit to regain her balance. She took four steps before doubling over again.

Nick was at her side immediately and frog-marched her back to the pallet. "Don't move," he commanded, not caring if she cursed at him again or not. "And don't argue either."

The answer to his earlier dilemma was clear now. He pulled a cell phone from his pocket, dialed and held it to his ear. "911? I have an emergency at the Do-It-Yourself Depot in Stone Mountain. Yes, that's the one. It's a very pregnant woman and I think she's in labor. Please hurry."

"I do not need to go to the hospital," Tess protested. "This is just practice contractions for the real thing. I'm fine. Really."

"Fine?" Well, yes, she was beyond fine in many respects, but her current situation was another matter. "You're what? Seven, eight months pregnant, waddling like a drunk penguin and obviously in a lot of pain. Why not just go to the ER and make sure everything is okay?"

"I told you. These are practice contractions. Something you'd know nothing about. I just need to get to my car and—"

By this time, both the store manager and the assistant manager had arrived on the scene. The store manager hovered nearby.

"I have someone posted at the front door to direct the paramedics right here to you. We'll make sure your wife and your baby get to the hospital as quickly as possible," the assistant manager assured Nick.

"I am not his wife," Tess responded defiantly through clenched teeth.

Nick's job had trained him to notice details, and while Tess had insisted she wasn't his wife, she had never said anything about the baby. Nick had already done the math in his head. If she was ready to deliver now, that meant she'd been pregnant the last time they'd had sex and never let on—if she had even known.

If she hadn't been pregnant then, that meant she was in premature labor, and a wave of apprehension grabbed at him like relentless undertow. He had watched enough cable TV to know this wasn't a good thing. It was even more imperative she get to a hospital as quickly as possible.

He closed his eyes, willed his body to relax and demanded his heart cease pounding and his brain stop imagining every negative scenario. He had to tamp down the panic for Tess's sake. And the baby's. If this was his baby—or even if it wasn't—he wanted to make sure it had every chance for survival, even if its mother was acting like an out-of-control banshee.

Within minutes the wail of sirens could be heard. Efficient paramedics loaded Tess onto a gurney and wheeled her, over her protests, to a waiting ambulance. Nick started to crawl in the back with her.

"Are you her husband?" the young, female paramedic asked.

Nick started to lie, but decided against it. Better not to get off on the wrong foot at this point. He shook his head.

"Then I can't allow you to ride along," the woman advised.

"Where are you taking her? I'll follow you."

Tess tried to sit up on the gurney in protest.

22

"Please lie still, ma'am." The second paramedic wrapped a blood pressure cuff around her arm, and she gently pushed against Tess's shoulder.

"Go home, Nick. Or go buy whatever you came here to buy. I am not your problem."

"Maybe not," he said. Or maybe she was; that was yet to be determined. "But I'm coming along anyway because you don't need to be alone. And don't argue."

The paramedic called out the hospital name as she stepped up into the back of the ambulance and pulled the doors closed.

Nick ran through the parking lot to his decade-old gray Range Rover, jammed the key into the ignition and turned it, the engine roaring to life. He slammed the column shifter into reverse and peeled rubber out of the parking lot, racing toward the hospital as he tried to keep the ambulance in sight. He wondered if anyone had called Tess's family. He knew her mother lived somewhere in the Atlanta area. He and Tess had usually been too busy in bed to talk much about their relatives and had never reached the step of swapping family addresses and phone numbers. That information had never seemed relevant—until now.

He would deal with that later, but first he had to call his own family and give them some reason for not returning with the varnish and drawer pulls.

Hey, Mom and Dad. I'm not sure when I'll be home. I might have knocked up a woman I've been sleeping with off and on for a couple years and she's in labor now. Gotta run.

Oh yeah, that would go over great with Ben and Carol Russo. They were gracious enough to let him live in the carriage house behind their home, and it provided the perfect housing for a bachelor who was only in town briefly every few months. But he didn't need to flaunt his sex life in their face—not yet anyway. Maybe he should just call his mother's cell phone. More than likely she wouldn't have it in the basement workshop where they had been working on the sideboard, and he could just leave a message.

Hi, Mom. I ran into an old friend at the hardware store and am following the ambulance to the hospital right now. My friend started feeling bad in the store and needed someone to go along for help. I'll call you later and let you know more.

Better. It contained no references to the nature of the hospital visit, the gender of the friend in question or the fact he'd had sex with this friend. He practiced several times before calling. He released a sigh of relief when he got his mother's voice mail, and he left the somewhat cryptic message, hoping it would be quite some time before she got around to checking it. By then he hoped he would be able to tell her…something. He wasn't sure what he'd say, but he would deal with that hurdle later.

Within minutes of dropping his cell onto the passenger seat, he had reached the hospital. He navigated the expansive multi-level parking structure, finally maneuvering the Range Rover into an empty space near the top level. He shifted into park then made a beeline for the emergency room entrance.

He rushed through the doors and saw the paramedics wheel Tess past the admissions desk and start down a long hallway.

Nick scrubbed his hand across the back of his neck and wondered just what in hell he'd gotten himself into. Too many questions pinged through his brain, one big question in particular, and he wanted answers. He just hoped he could get Tess to provide them.

Chapter Three

Nick sat back, watching as a fortyish man in a white coat scrutinized lab reports on a computer screen in the corner of the sterile hospital room. Earlier, he had introduced himself earlier as Dr. Merrell, Tess's obstetrician.

"Tess, you're a lucky woman. If you hadn't come in when you did, your son might have made an early entrance and caused us even more problems. You're also lucky you chose a hospital with a neonatal ICU for delivery and you were close to it when you started having problems."

"I thought it was just—"

"Braxton Hicks. Yes, you told me. But they don't cause pain bad enough to double you over. Additionally, your blood pressure is elevated, which probably accounts for the headache you had. Your feet and ankles are swollen more than normal for the third trimester too. I warned you at your last visit that you were working too hard and needed to take it easy. Have you thought about my suggestion that you ask for early maternity leave? It's really not a suggestion any more. Because of today's episode and your age, it's a necessity, both for the sake of your health and that of your baby."

It all sounded like mumbo jumbo to Nick—except the part about the baby being a boy. If he had he heard the term Braxton Hicks anywhere else, he'd have assumed it was in reference to a country music singer. But he wasn't surprised that Tess was working hard. She was career driven for sure.

"I'm sure if I just go home and rest for the remainder of the weekend I'll be fine by Monday." Tess pushed herself to a sitting position and started to swing her legs over the side of the hospital bed.

"If you leave this hospital right now, it will be against medical advice, and I can tell you now that if something happens and your insurance company sees AMA on your records they could refuse to pay any medical claims." The doctor's tone was firm and no-nonsense. "Do you have hundreds of thousands of dollars to cover neonatal intensive care costs out of pocket if you give birth prematurely?"

Tess shoved her legs back under the covers and laid back against the bed, giving a little sigh of defeat. She gnawed her lower lip, which quivered slightly. "I can't stay in here indefinitely. I have a job, and I don't have any family here to help me out."

The look of helplessness on her face tugged at Nick. He knew how much Tess valued her independence. He also knew just how strong-willed she was. And now her unborn baby's health had been placed in the crosshairs of those two traits.

Dr. Merrell raised one eyebrow and shifted his gaze in Nick's direction. And Nick quickly shifted his gaze to a spot on the vinyl floor beside the toe of his left shoe. He didn't want to be around a woman who had unceremoniously dumped him without an explanation. But her pregnant belly raised a few questions; one in particular. Did the child she was carrying belong to him?

If not, then he could walk away with a completely clear conscience, knowing he'd done his good deed for the day by insisting she go to the hospital.

If the baby *was* his, why hadn't she let him know? If the baby was his, how could he walk away and turn his back on Tess? On his own child?

His son.

"You'll have to figure out something, and you need to figure it out soon. We've stabilized you, and the baby is in no immediate danger. I'm going to recommend you stay overnight, maybe two so we're sure things stay steady. Use that time to make some arrangements for help at home and at work, and if I'm convinced it's safe, I'll release you. But if I see you're overdoing it again, I'll stick you back in that hospital bed." Dr. Merrell's tone made it clear his terms were non-negotiable.

"How am I supposed to finish getting ready for this baby to arrive if I'm stuck in bed at home?" Tess asked in an exasperated tone. "I have a to-do list as long as my arm, and I had planned on having two more months to complete it."

"You won't have to actually stay in bed, but you have to lower your stress levels, especially at work, and you can't do anything physically strenuous like housework or yard work." The doctor referred to the computer screen again. "Or assembling furniture. Get someone to help you with that."

Once again the doctor eyed Nick, who was already feeling twinges of guilt over the snide comments he'd made when he and Tess had literally run into each other. Sure, she'd looked like she was having trouble, but goading her with sexist comments probably hadn't helped.

Maybe he could somehow make amends for that, if Tess didn't let her stubborn streak and her obvious disdain for him get in the way.

"Meanwhile, I need to examine you again. Would you like Mr....uhm...?"

"Russo," Nick said. "Nick Russo."

"Would you like Mr. Russo to stay or not?"

Tess gave the doctor a deer-in-the-headlights look. "Not. Oh, most definitely not."

Nick smothered a grin because he'd already seen everything the doctor was going to look at—on numerous occasions. He pushed himself off the straight-back chair where he had been sitting for the past hour once Tess had okayed his being there in her room.

"This won't take long, so why don't you go to the cafeteria and get yourself something to eat?" The doctor gave Nick a sympathetic look, which made Nick wonder if he knew who the baby's father was.

Why won't someone let me in on the secret?

"I'll just...whatever," Nick said as he ambled from the room. Maybe he'd do a little more than get food. Perhaps a peace offering was in order.

*****

Tess shifted in the hospital bed, adjusting her pillow and crinkling her nose against the smell of Betadine, which permeated the air. Beside her bed, a fetal monitor beeped and blinked, displaying her son's vital signs, indicating he was healthy and strong. Seven hours had passed since she had been moved from the emergency room to the obstetrical floor, and she was bored silly. She was used to staying busy all day and half the night. Her fault. She heaved a sign of resignation. If she had just listened to the doctor she wouldn't be here now. Beating herself up over her stubbornness was pointless. The damage had been done and all she could do now was follow the doctor's orders and make sure she delivered a healthy baby when he was due and not before.

But what was she going to do now that she'd been ordered to take it easy? She already had a lawn service, and she could hire someone to keep house and cook. But what about her job? Her caseload? The clients who depended on her? Her plan had been to work until a week before her due date, which was eight weeks away. Her calendar for the next seven weeks held the Wilsons' mediation, Ronald Patterson's appeal brief, four modification trials on the same docket, and several new divorce clients who needed counsel on their options.

Tears of frustration filled her eyes. If she followed the doctor's orders, she would let her clients down. But if she didn't, she would put her child at risk. As much as she valued her work, the baby growing inside her had to be her top priority.

When the pregnancy test had been positive, Tess had tried to call Nick. She had no idea if he was in the country or halfway around the world. His cell phone worked everywhere. When her call rolled to his voice mail, she hung up because this wasn't the kind of news you left in an impersonal message. Two days later she had tried to call again, then a week after that. Each time she heard his voice mail greeting and each time she disconnected without leaving a message.

He never returned her calls though he should have known from the caller ID she was the caller. She'd felt a twinge of hurt and anger over his lack of communication but knew she had no claim on Nick Russo, even though his child was growing inside her. And she most definitely wasn't looking for a husband or a handout.

She could take care of herself and her baby. Her own mother's circumstances had drilled the concept of self-sufficiency into Tess from an early age. She'd vowed never to make herself dependent on a man for anything. Ever.

In the two years they had known each other, Nick had called her every three to four months, whenever his job brought him back to Atlanta. But it had been nearly eight months since she'd seen him—since that last night of endless orgasms. She had presumed he'd lost interest in her, and she refused to pursue a man who wasn't interested in her, baby or not.

She might feel a bit desperate with regard to her job, but not that desperate. She had seen too many women marry for the wrong reasons and end up in her office seeking to dissolve the marriage when the relationship went sour.

"Time to check your vitals," a cheery voice sounded from behind the curtain shielding her bed from the doorway. An older nurse pushed the curtain aside and a look of concern crossed her face when she reached Tess's side and saw the tears streaking her face. "Are you in pain, Ms. Callahan? Should I call the doctor?"

Tess raised one hand to swipe at the tears before remembering the IV line taped to the back of it. "No pain. Just a little pity party."

"Here you go, dear," the nurse said, snapping several tissues from the box on the bedside table and pressing them into Tess's free hand. "Are you sure you aren't hurting? We wouldn't want anything to happen to that little fellow in there. Is there anyone I can call for you? Your mother perhaps? A sister or a friend?"

Tess dabbed at the tears and shook her head. "I don't have any brothers or sisters. My mother has Alzheimer's and lives in a special facility so there's no point in trying to call her."

"What about a good friend then?"

Tess had been so busy making a living that she'd never taken the time to make much of a life for herself. She had one good friend in the world, but Maddie Worth and her husband Jack had two small daughters, the younger one just three months old. Tess couldn't ask them to babysit her when they were busy with their own family.

"I can't ask her to help me. She has her own small children to take care of." Asking for help had never been Tess's forte. Would she have gone to Maddie for help even if she didn't have a family to care for?

"Maybe so, but I'll bet she can take some time to just talk on the phone," the nurse suggested. "And what about that nice young man who came in with you? He seemed very concerned about you and the baby. I came in while you were napping this afternoon and I don't think he took his eyes off that fetal monitor the whole time I was in the room."

"Well…he…we…" Tess gave a resigned shrug and dabbed at her eyes again.

The nurse took the cue, unintended as it was. She quickly checked Tess, recorded the results and then moved toward the door.

"Think about calling your friend," she urged as she paused in the doorway. "She just might surprise you." With that advice hanging in the air, she left.

Tess glanced at the wall clock and noted the time. She picked up the phone and hoped Maddie would forgive her for calling after the girls' bedtime.

After two rings her friend answered with a tentative hello.

"Maddie? I'm sorry to call so late but—"

"Tess, what's wrong? The caller ID shows the hospital." Concern vibrated in Maddie's usually steady voice.

"It's nothing really. A little hiccup with the pregnancy, but Dr. Merrell is making me stay here for at least one night. Maybe two. But it's no big deal."

"No big deal? You forget who you're talking to. I've had two babies, remember? Hang on." Tess heard Maddie's hushed tones as she explained to her husband that Tess was on the other end of the line. "Jack says hi. Now, fess up. The doctor didn't put you in the hospital just for grins and giggles. What's wrong? I can hear the fetal monitor in the background."

"Remember the chest I ordered for the nursery? I went to buy a screwdriver for it, was insulted by the Misogynist of the Year and kinda started having some contractions just before I almost literally ran into Nick." She left out the part about how safe she'd felt in Nick's arms and how close she'd come to telling him the baby was his. The man deserved to know the truth. She wasn't quite ready to tell him, and she had no idea *how* to break the news. He probably knew--or at least suspected—given how attentive he had been all day.

"Interesting. The part about Nick, that is."

"Yeah. Of all the stores in all the suburbs in all of Atlanta…" She cut the *Casablanca* reference short. "So now I'm stuck in a hospital bed feeling an awful lot like Frankenstein's monster with all these tubes and wires everywhere. The doctor even threatened he might keep me until the baby comes. I can't stay here. What about my clients? And my mother? I'm her emotional anchor and she won't understand if I can't visit regularly." Tess watched the heart rate display on the fetal monitor increase in speed, which meant her agitation was probably causing her baby distress as well.

She took a deep breath, let it hiss out between her teeth and willed herself to relax so the entire obstetrics staff would not come rushing into the room armed for an emergency.

"What's wrong? Are you doing Lamaze breathing? Is something the matter?" Maddie's worried questions came in rapid fire succession.

"I'm not in labor…yet. But the doctor hinted that if I don't take it easy I could go into labor early. Oh, God, Maddie. Why did I think I could do this alone? I must be out of my ever-loving mind." Tess shivered as her control began to slip, and a new level of apprehension swept over her in waves.

"Probably for the same reason I thought I could do it alone too," Maddie reminded her. "And that's not meant to be derogatory in any way. I had different circumstances than you—"

"And you ended up with absolutely the world's best husband."

Maddie, who practiced law at the same firm as Tess, initially had chosen to have a baby through artificial insemination after her first husband died at a young age before they'd had a chance to start a family. When she got a reality check on single motherhood, she agreed to marry Jack in the convoluted belief that they would have a marriage of convenience. Ha! Talk about true love affairs.

"Yeah, I did." Maddie paused a few moments before speaking again. "Have you talked to Nick about this? I mean really talked and explained everything? The man has a right to know he's going to be a father, and who knows? He might step up and offer to help you."

"Or he might not, and I'd rather not have to suffer that embarrassment if he doesn't. Maddie, I tried to call him and he never called back."

"Did you leave him a message?" Maddie asked pointedly.

"No. But when he saw three missed calls from me he should have figured something was up and returned my calls."

"Don't get me wrong. I love Jack with all my heart. But I learned early on that he isn't a mind reader. If I want him to know something, I have to spell it right out for him. Sometimes I think the man needs an engraved invitation handed to him on a silver platter so he'll know exactly what I need from him."

"Well, I don't love Nick," Tess replied.

Liar, her conscience screamed. Her feelings toward Nick had begun to change during the last weekend they'd spent together, and when she'd found out she was pregnant, she had even had a few dreams of picket fences and happily ever after. More than a few if she admitted the truth. The un-returned phone calls had burst that bubble into a million pieces and sent her life careening in another direction.

"You don't have to love him, sweetie, but I still say the man deserves to know the baby is his. Are you sure he hasn't already done the math and figured it out for himself?"

Tess had asked herself the same question a dozen times since that afternoon. And after the nurse's comment about him staring at the fetal monitor while she napped, maybe he *did* suspect. He'd been awfully attentive for a friend with benefits, unless he had deduced an extra benefit—or liability—might exist

"I'll think about telling him," she replied with hesitation.

"Think about it. Think about it hard, Tess. What if he decides to assert his parental rights? Do you want your personal life played out in a public courtroom?

"He wouldn't do that."

"Are you sure?"

"You know as well as I that most unwed mothers never collect a dime of child support from—"

"That isn't what I asked," Maddie interrupted. "Do you want a judge making decisions about your life and your child's life?"

Tess released a sigh. "No, I don't. That's usually not an optimal outcome."

"Then you need to make some decisions soon," Maddie emphasized. "And get some rest. Take advantage of having everyone wait on you hand and foot because after the baby comes you won't get to rest for a while." A loud yawn was audible over the phone. "A long, long while."

"I promise I'll rest. I don't have much choice, actually. They practically have me handcuffed to the bed with armed guards at every door."

"You, handcuffed to the bed. Now that sure brings back some memories," a deep male voice said from just beyond the privacy curtain.

"I need to go. Nick's here," Tess muttered into the phone.

"So I heard. Does he look anywhere near as sexy as his voice sounds?"

Tess hesitated and contemplated whether to answer.

"Does he?" Maddie's courtroom cross-examination tone had crept into her voice.

"Yes. And I'm hanging up now."

"Bye, sweetie. Let me know if I can do anything. And talk to him," Maddie urged again before hanging up.

Tess returned the phone to its cradle. She had often thought of Nick as sex on a stick. And now she had practically admitted the same to her best friend. She also had to take Maddie's advice to heart.

She looked up to see Nick step into the room with a tall plastic cup in one hand and a vase of flowers in the other. He placed the vase on the bedside table and, grabbing a straw off the hospital bed tray, peeled the paper wrapping off before jabbing it through the opening in the cup's lid.

"I thought you might like a chocolate shake about now," he said, offering her the cup. "I remembered it's your favorite. And I hope you like daisies."

The simple bouquet caused a lone tear to trickle down her cheek.

"I can take them away if you don't," he stammered, his outstretched hand pulling back. "The grocery store down the street is a little low on floral varieties this time of night."

Tess did some rapid blinking.

Damn hormones.

"I love daisies," she admitted. She slid the straw between her lips, sucked up a mouthful of heaven then let out a slow "Ahhhh."

Another long sip elicited a delighted moan as the cold treat slid down her throat. And damn Nick for remembering chocolate milkshakes were her favorite late-night indulgence. The same hormones that one moment made her cry over the thoughtful gesture and made her want to hate him the next. She needed to hate him for not returning her calls, but how could she when he brought her flowers and chocolate?

She sucked another mouthful of milkshake from the cup then stopped herself before she held out the cup and asked if he wanted to share; that's what they had often done during their times together. Hot sex followed by a cold milkshake and then a trip to Do-It-Yourself Depot to look for supplies for whatever project he was working on.

But she was supposed to be hating him now, not taking a trip down memory lane.

Nick shrugged out of his leather jacket and settled into the chair he had vacated earlier. Whiskers shadowed his jaw and his dark hair was disheveled as if he'd repeatedly run his hands through it.

As she finished the milkshake Tess noticed his dark gaze wander to her abdomen and then anxiously shift to the fetal monitor.

Damn Maddie too. The man *did* have the right to know he was going to be a father. Maybe she had allowed her independent streak to go a little too far. Maybe Nick had been in some remote section of Borneo without cell phone reception and that's why he hadn't returned her calls. Maybe he had been on assignment in the farthest corner of Siberia where there were few towns and cell phone towers were unheard of. Maybe he'd been gone the entire time since they'd spent their last night together.

"We have something we need to talk about," she said cautiously and gauged Nick's reaction. Sure enough, he looked at the monitor again. He scrubbed his fingers across the back of his neck then ran them through his hair, causing the wayward locks to become even more tousled.

He crossed his arms defensively and leaned back in the chair. "I'm all ears." His tone was cool and even.

Maybe she could get through this without crying.

She waved a hand over her stomach. "I guess you were a little surprised to see me like this." Her voice faltered. She reached for a glass of water on the tray and took a long drink.

His dark eyebrows raised inquiringly above espresso-colored eyes that remained trained on her face. "Oh yeah. More than a little. Surprised is an understatement."

"And I guess you're wondering how this happened, huh?"

"I think it's pretty obvious how it happened, but there's a question that's really burning in my mind right now. Actually it's been burning there since I saw you this afternoon."

He never said the words, but Tess knew what they were, and the time had arrived to come clean about everything.

Tess placed her hand gently on her abdomen and looked directly at him. "This is your baby, Nick."

He nodded. "I pretty much suspected it was, but I don't know whether to be excited or mad or confused."

She could understand the first two reactions. But the third? "Confused?"

"Well, I did use a condom. Every single time," he said with a hint of irritation in his voice. "I take that responsibility seriously."

"You know as well as I do they're not foolproof. Nothing is foolproof. Abstinence is the only method that's one hundred percent effective to prevent pregnancy, and I don't seem to remember either one of us being a great big fan of that." Tess felt the baby kick as if to tell her to calm down. "I didn't date anyone while you were gone. I can have DNA tests run if you…" Her voice trailed off and she looked away, avoiding his gaze altogether.

"No, there's no need for that. I have no reason to doubt you. I do wonder why you didn't tell me, but we'll table that discussion for the time being. However, I am concerned about you not taking the doctor's advice. This is serious business, Tess. That's our son who's at risk." He gestured toward the monitor that displayed the baby's vital signs. "Since I'm between assignments, I'm going to help you."

Tess lost her battle against the tears, and Nick was beside her in two strides. He sat on the edge of the bed and used his thumb to wipe away the tears. Then he leaned over and kissed her gently on the cheek.

"If the doctor will release you from the hospital, I'll stay with you until you can hire someone to come in and help. Is that a workable solution?"

Tess nodded, unable to speak around the lump in her throat.

"You worry about everything else, and I'll put the chest together," Nick offered. "After all, I do have every conceivable screwdriver known to man."

"Thank you. I'd like that very much."

Tess heard him chuckle softly. "That had to hurt, Tessie. You accepting help from someone had to hurt a damned lot. I was afraid you might tell me to go to hell again."

"Don't tempt me."

Chapter Four

Seatbelts and baby bumps were not compatible. Tess tugged and shifted until she was as comfortable as she would ever be with the three-point harness wrapped around her and her bulging belly.

What had she been thinking? Having Nick stay at her place was not a good idea. It was quite possibly the worst idea in the world, but at the moment, she was pretty much out of other options. From her hospital room, she had called several agencies that provided home care aides, and she had interviews scheduled with two possible candidates once she got settled in at home.

She glanced to her left and watched Nick grip the steering wheel with both hands and drive a conservative ten miles per hour below the posted speed limit. It seemed as if he wanted her encased in bubble wrap before buckling her into the front seat.

"You can drive the speed limit, Nick. Traffic is backing up behind us and this time of day is the after-school rush—"

Nick glanced in her direction, and the glare he delivered cut her short. The issue of accepting help was new territory for Tess, and she had to make it work. She also had to figure out Nick's thoughts about the baby. The rather dramatic way he had learned of his impending fatherhood had to grate on him. But now wasn't the time to ask him outright. She would have to ease into that question. But drama or not, her mind buzzed as she speculated over his feelings.

When they turned into the driveway of the large Colonial home where, she had learned, Nick had grown up, the sun was past the midway point in the sky. The doctor had done rounds while Tess waited anxiously to be discharged, but Dr. Merrell hadn't given the okay for Tess to be released until two o'clock. She knew the doctor wanted her to stay in the hospital for another night, but she had begged to go home to the comfort of her own bed and promised the doctor she would rest. Nick's assurances that he would enforce the doctor's ordered convinced Dr. Merrell to sign her release papers and let her leave.

Tall oak trees filled the yard in front of the house, and landscaped beds of neatly trimmed shrubbery lined the sidewalks and perimeter of the house. Tess's life had begun in similar surroundings, but those surroundings hadn't lasted like they had with Nick's family.

Nick drove to the back and pulled up to the carriage house located at the rear of the property. Nick lived in an apartment on the second floor and used the ground level as a darkroom. Tess had been there a few times, when it had been quicker to get to his bed than to hers. His living quarters were Spartan, not because he didn't care, but because a man who traveled most of the time just didn't have time to turn a house into a home.

Tess's apartment had been better furnished, but only because she had hired someone to do it. But it hadn't been a home. She had enjoyed living in the center of Atlanta, right in the middle of the action. But one trip to the Baby Super Center brought the stark realization that a one-bedroom apartment would not be adequate living quarters once the baby arrived. So after considering a move to a larger apartment, Tess conceded that her child deserved the suburban house, picket fence, big backyard kind of life. A life just like Nick had apparently experienced.

"You can wait here while I pack a few things," Nick said. "The doctor warned you about overdoing it and I don't want to risk you falling on these steps."

There he goes with the bubble wrap again.

"I deal with stairs every day, Nick. And I use the railing and I wear sensible shoes and I look both ways at the top and bottom—"

"Don't be a smart ass. It's not becoming of a woman in your…It's not becoming."

She stuck her tongue out at him. "I'll sit right here. Master," she added.

When he learned her bedroom was on the second floor of her new home, he would probably suggest she have an elevator installed. Or rearrange everything and turn her den into a bedroom, complete with a hospital bed and wheelchair.

Tess watched every muscle in his body flex as he took the steps two at a time. When she noticed movement out of the corner of her eye, she turned and saw two women lean their leaf rakes against the privacy fence surrounding the backyard and stare at the vehicle where she sat. One was older—most likely Nick's mother—and the other bore a strong resemblance to Nick. She guessed her to be one of the sisters Nick had mentioned on occasion.

The women spoke to each other, glancing back toward Tess a few times before retrieving their garden tools and resuming the pretense of raking leaves. Tess preferred stairs to stares, so she shouldered open the car door and swiveled out of the seat and to the ground. As she waddled to the staircase she realized she had just made a huge tactical error. Lord knows what conclusions these women would jump to when they saw Nick leave with a suitcase and a pregnant woman.

Tess had to laugh, though, because at least one conclusion was absolutely correct. If they *were* Nick's mother and sister, they'd soon find out they were going to become a grandmother and aunt, respectively.

She navigated the steps carefully then walked in through the door Nick had left open and surveyed the space. The apartment was much the same as she remembered, though most of her memories were made in the bedroom and shower.

She started to lower herself onto the overstuffed plaid sofa then had second thoughts. It might be comfortable, but she recalled it being low and deep, remembering other occasions where she'd had to struggle to get to her feet after sitting on it. Not pregnant. Her emotional state was fragile enough without a reminder she was as big as a barn and wore clothing that looked like it had been designed by a tent maker.

Nick walked out of the bedroom, a duffle bag in one hand and his camera case slung over one shoulder. He came up short when he saw Tess.

"Is something wrong?" he asked anxiously, setting the bags on his small dining table and moving to her side. "If you needed something you should have just blown the horn. I'd have come down instead of you climbing the steps. You know what the doctor said about what could happen if you—"

"Stop being such a mother hen," she interrupted with exasperation. "And no, nothing is wrong. Well, truthfully, I just got a little bit uncomfortable with those women out there staring at me and whispering to each other. A *lot* uncomfortable to be precise."

Nick walked to the doorway, looked out and waved.

"That's my mother and my sister Bella." He chewed his lip nervously. "You know they're going to ask questions since they saw…your condition."

"I don't have a condition. A condition is something like pink eye or toenail fungus. I'm pregnant, Nick. This is the twenty-first century and it's okay to say the word in mixed company."

His jaw clenched, then relaxed. "I can tell them you're someone I know from the magazine and—"

"Don't lie to them, Nick," she pleaded. "Honestly. I should have tried harder to get in touch with you when I found out I was pregnant. I called several times but didn't want to tell you about the baby in a voice message. Hell, I could have called *them* and asked how to get in touch with you. But I was scared and confused, and the longer I waited, the more difficult it became to face reality as far as you were concerned. Everything just snowballed out of control until it was easier to ignore it than deal with the truth."

"Yeah, I can imagine. It's not like we had any sort of a commitment thing going on. I mean, it was just sex with no promises of anything except a good time. And I was always careful, but as you said, nothing is foolproof." His gaze darted to the doorway. "I did see that you had called, but since you didn't leave a message, I figured it was nothing important."

Tess remembered her lie to Maddie two days before.

I don't love Nick.

And his comment reinforced that he didn't love her—that she had merely been a friend with benefits arrangement for him, which, up until their last time together, has been true for her too. She'd been a good time when he was in town, and though she wouldn't ask, she suspected a handsome man like Nick probably had a lot of good times scattered around the world. He was the sort of man any woman would fall for.

Even though love and relationships had been the furthest thing from her mind, she had to admit, falling for Nick was a kick in her self-sufficient, no-strings-attached backside.

She would just accept his gracious offer of assistance—or was the offer driven by guilt?—and hire some household help as quickly as possible. Then she could ease Nick back out of her life and get that life back to normal, whatever "normal" was going to be from now on.

"Come on. I need to get you home and in bed."

"And where have I heard that line before?" Tess joked.

Nick nudged her in the rear with his knee. "As I said before, don't be a smart ass. It isn't becoming for a woman in your condi— a preg— It isn't becoming. I'll take my stuff to the car and then come back and help you to the car."

"I am not an invalid. I made it up and I can get back down," she said in a huff. "But can we make a fast getaway so I don't have to talk to your family just yet?"

Nick peered through the open door again. "They've gone inside, no doubt to call my father and see if he knows anything about the pregnant woman his son just drove up with."

"I don't want to cause you any problems with your family." The tears began again, and Tess gave in to them. It was difficult not to cry and feel sorry for herself when she'd made such a mess of her life and perhaps put her baby's life in danger too.

*****

Nick pulled her into his arms. He never had forgotten the feel of her; while her swollen belly kept him from pulling her close, she still smelled like sunshine and felt like magic in his arms. Tucking her head under his chin and feeling her heart beat against his chest kicked his ticker into high gear. The baby forced a sideways hug, but awkward as it was, holding Tess felt wonderful.

They were a good fit in more ways than one, and he willed his body not to react to the memories of how fantastic they had been in bed.

Tess had been an inventive and adventurous lover. She was comfortable with her body and appreciative of his. Damned appreciative, and his cock twitched at the memory of a silk scarf, some scented massage oil and—

He wrenched his thoughts from that memory. Tess needed assistance now, not some randy man. She had admitted in her hospital room that she hadn't been with another man since the last time they had been together. Perhaps he should admit he hadn't been with anyone else either. There was no shame in self-imposed celibacy.

"I'll deal with my family," he reassured her. "We're Italian. We're used to drama."

"And I feel like I've been the poster child for drama queens the past few days. I don't like being this way, but these damn—"

"Hormones," he interjected and then rested his chin on the top of her head, catching a whiff of her floral-scented shampoo. "I know. One of my sisters has thirteen-year-old twin daughters. I remember things got quite lively when she was pregnant. Between my mother, my two sisters, my brother's wife and Angie's daughters, let's just say our family get-togethers are a real estrogen fest."

"Is that what I am? An estrogen fest?" She sniffled and Nick heard her voice catch in her throat.

He stepped back and studied her, starting at her spiky mop of sun-streaked brown hair and stopping at her eyes, which were as green as emeralds. Tears caused them to sparkle like the finest of gems, but Nick could live a lifetime without that sort of sparkle.

Those eyes had captured his interest the night he had met her at a costume party two years before. She had worn a white dress with a sexy deep neckline. Wicked strappy do-me high heels added several inches to her already tall frame and had him fantasizing about those shapely legs being wrapped around him.

When they had stepped out onto the ballroom's balcony overlooking the city, the wind had whipped her skirt up and she let out a raucous laugh while she patted it back into place. He realized the significance of her costume at that moment. Her hair was completely different from the blonde Hollywood bombshell's both in color and style, but she had a strategically placed beauty mark above her left lip—a mark he'd kissed off before midnight.

God, yes, she *was* an estrogen fest complete with hormonal horror, maudlin mayhem and bitchy bedlam, and all of it would be sure to keep him in a constant state of anxiety. He had to hide that, though, and make sure she remained calm and carried the baby—his baby—for as long as possible.

Nick pulled her back against him and pressed his lips to hers. He wanted to deepen the kiss, but resisted. Now wasn't the time for arousal because they could no longer run off to bed and douse the fires of passion. Offering to move in and help until she found someone else to assist her was merely doing what was right, but he had no business getting romantically involved with Tess. So he'd better learn to keep his body in check.

Her lips softened against his and a soft moan slipped from between them. He was hard in an instant.

So much for keeping the body in check, you ass.

In the past, he would have taken her right then. Picked her up and carried her straight to bed. If this was any indication of how much she still affected him, Nick imagined he would be taking lots of cold showers in the next couple of days.

He ended the kiss abruptly. "Come on. I need to get you home before you get too tired."

Tess's eyes fluttered open and she grabbed the back of a chair to steady herself. Then her gaze traveled slowly from his face down the length of his body and lingered at his crotch for a few seconds before shifting back to his face. A perceptive grin curved her mouth.

Damn. Busted.

With a nervous cough Nick shouldered his duffel and camera bag and helped Tess take the steps one at a time. At the hospital, an orderly had helped get her into the SUV. Now it was just the two of them, and he was wishing he'd paid closer attention to how the orderly maneuvered her into the passenger seat.

"Hold onto my shoulders," he suggested. "Let me lift you." He reached for her waist and realized she no longer had one. He studied her body to find some other place to grab hold of her, and then peered over his shoulder to see if his mother and sister were watching from the window.

Wouldn't that be a riot?

Seeing no faces at any of the back windows, he first placed one hand on her ass before figuring out that method wouldn't work. With one smooth move, he put one hand around her shoulders, the other under her knees and simply scooped her into his arms and placed her into the Range Rover.

"I can't wait to take a shower and get into some other clothes," she said after Nick had positioned himself behind the steering wheel. "I feel like I've been in these things forever. And I need to get my car from Do-It-Yourself Depot too, if they haven't already had it impounded."

"I called the store manager and explained, and he said it wasn't a problem. He's even going to have his security guys keep an eye on it. I'll get my dad to drive it to your place."

Nick backed out of the drive and wove his way out of his parents' old, established neighborhood. He'd ridden his bicycle through these streets as a kid, climbed the trees in their front yard and caught frogs in the creek nearby. Would his son be able to do those things too? He frowned, remembering the small apartment where Tess lived. No trees, busy traffic all around and definitely no creek.

When he reached the main thoroughfare, he turned and headed in the direction of downtown Atlanta. "I'm going to take the back roads to your apartment since the interstate is a nightmare this time of day. It'll take us longer but I don't want to add to your stress level."

"Apartment? I don't live in the apartment anymore. I have a house in Tucker. I'm having a baby in case you didn't notice and I'm going to need more than one bedroom."

"Okay, well…"

Tess squinted at him with a slightly annoyed look on her face. "If you thought I was still in my apartment, just where did you think you were going to sleep? With me?"

Nick opened his mouth to reply, but Tess continued, clearly on a tear. "If you think you're sharing my bed, think again, buster. This baby and I have enough trouble getting comfortable without an extra body taking up space in the bed, even if it is a king. You're lucky I have a furnished guest room or you'd be in a sleeping bag in a tent in my backyard."

Nick held up one hand in a gesture of surrender. "Just tell me how to get to this house of yours and we'll sort out the sleeping arrangements once we get there."

Tess snorted. "There's no sorting about it. Junior and I sleep alone. Well, as alone as… Oh, screw it."

Nick bit back a laugh. "You know you're going to have to tame that tongue of yours. Haven't you heard the phrase *little pitchers have big ears*?"

"Just drive," she ordered as she leaned her head against the headrest and closed her eyes.

Twenty minutes later, Nick pulled into the driveway of a two-story, white-frame home situated on a cul-de-sac in a modest neighborhood. The house and yard were well kept and appealing. A front porch spanned the width of the house and had a rocking chair and a swing–a nice place to relax on a pleasant evening. The lot had mature trees and he had seen other children playing in yards all along the street. He was reminded of his own childhood.

"Which way is your bedroom?" he asked after getting her out of the car, a task far easier than the reverse.

"The stairs are this way," she began.

"Stairs? Your bedroom is upstairs? Oh, no. we'll have to move you to a downstairs bedroom. Well, not we—you and me. I'll get my pop to help. You can't be hauling ass—"

"Stop right there, mister potty mouth." She crossed her arms, a motion that drew attention to her breasts, which were larger than Nick remembered. "First, I do not remember the doctor specifically banning stairs. He said for me to take it easy. And second, there isn't a bedroom downstairs."

"Then we'll… I'll rent a hospital bed and set up your den as a bedroom. You do have a den, don't you?"

"Yes, but there's only a powder room down here. No shower. I guess you could rent a big wash tub too and heat water on the stove for me, but if I ever got into it, you'd have to rent a crane to lift me out.

He closed his eyes and pursed his lips. "Point taken. I'll carry you up—"

She held up one hand to silence him, and Nick knew when to surrender.

"Can I at least walk up the stairs behind you in case you lose your balance?"

"Don't be a smart ass."

"Isn't that my line?"

"You won't have a line or anything else if you don't can it."

He kept vigil outside the bathroom door while she showered and dressed. When she emerged from the bathroom, she wore a demure, flower-print nightgown that hung loose and fell to her ankles. He was quite sure it wasn't part of the Victoria's Secret collection.

"What's the matter? Have you never seen a granny gown before?" she asked as she towel-dried her hair.

Yes. On his granny. But he certainly wasn't going to tell her that. This nightwear contrasted sharply with what she had worn the nights they'd spent together. Or more accurately, the nightwear he had taken off her the nights they'd spent together.

He struggled for an appropriate response. Was this what the next few days would be like? A never-ending walking on egg shells?

"I'm sure it's comfortable," he replied.

A wistful look crossed her face. "Yeah, it's comfortable, but it's so much easier to intimidate a hostile witness in a navy power suit and stilettos than a maternity dress and shoes so ugly the fashion police would have me indicted."

She sighed heavily and waddled across the room. He settled her into bed, where she propped herself against the headboard, a book on childbirth spread on her lap. Within minutes, she fell asleep.

He'd have to remember to borrow that book, or buy his own copy, in case she wanted him with her when the baby arrived. He'd like to witness the birth, but ultimately, it was up to Tess whether or not she was going to allow that to happen. He would argue his case, but he wasn't sure of his rights since they weren't married. He didn't know if he could demand to be in the delivery room. If not, he'd have to accept that fact and try like hell to convince her otherwise before her due date.

He retrieved his belongings from the Range Rover and placed them in the guest room, which was down the hall from Tess's room. As a photographer, he had an eye for people and their surroundings and had done some interior design photography several years earlier for friends opening a design firm. Tess's bedroom could have come straight from their showroom. Her apartment had been more a mixture of styles and colors designed for utility. This room with its king-sized bed with a white wood headboard and matching nightstands lacked personality. Where was the Tess he knew?

A self-guided tour of the rest of the house was in order. The upstairs contained another full bathroom and a smaller bedroom next to the master. From the unassembled chest and stacks of other baby things, he presumed this was going to be the baby's nursery. Samples of several colors of paint chips were taped to one wall and a magazine photo of a baby's room was taped to the window frame. The pieces of the chest of drawers that had precipitated the events of the last few days lay strewn in one corner. Two other boxes, one containing the pieces for a crib and the other a changing table, were stacked against one wall.

Lots of work remained to be done if the room was to be ready by her due date. And what if, despite all their precautions, the baby arrived early? Nick had heard tales of babies sleeping in dresser drawers and laundry baskets. His son might not care where he slept, but Nick sure did.

He slipped downstairs quietly and helped himself to a tall glass of milk and a couple of cookies from a package lying on the kitchen countertop before wandering through the other downstairs rooms. The rest of the house seemed cozy enough, but nothing of Tess jumped out at him. That made him wonder where the Tess he'd spent so much time with had disappeared to. Where was the woman with panache and a take-no-prisoners attitude? The woman who could cuss like a sailor one minute and whisper sexy innuendo in his ear the next?

Nick carried the milk and cookies to the front porch and settled into the swing to contemplate how his life had been upended in the last forty-eight hours. He pushed his foot against the porch floor to set the swing in motion and had settled back when his cell phone vibrated in his jeans pocket.

The caller ID indicated it was his sister Bella, and for a moment he contemplated letting the call roll to voice mail. The last thing he wanted now was an interrogation. He knew Bella and his mother had seen Tess in all her pregnant glory and had been whispering to each other. Hell, he didn't even know all the answers, so what could he tell Bella? But, he answered, knowing exactly what she'd ask and that he'd have to deal with her and his mother sooner or later.

"Hey, Bella."

"Do you have something you want to tell me, Nicky?"

"The weather in Sydney is damn near perfect in February, but I believe I could live a lifetime without seeing someone eat grubs and goanna. I mean, Crocodile Dundee is alive and well in Oz even today. I got some great shots, the boss is pleased and—"

"I love the travelogue and can't wait to see the article, but you know what I'm asking about." Her voice held that big-sister tone of authority he hated as much as he hated the nickname she'd used. Regret over answering the phone already settled in his gut.

He took in a long breath and exhaled slowly. "Yep, I do. But I'd rather talk to Mom and Pop together and explain everything to them all at one time."

Once I know everything there is to explain.

"Okay, that's understandable. I'm still at the house, so I'll get them on the speaker phone and you can explain away."

"No," Nick said forcefully. "I mean, I'll explain everything, but I'd rather do it in person. I can't get back to the house until at least tomorrow, maybe the day after. Do you think y'all can wait until then?"

"Why can't you come sooner?" Nick detected a hint of exasperation in her voice. "Mom and I know what we saw and we're dying to know where you were going with a suitcase and a woman who looked like she was ready to give birth any moment."

Anger and annoyance grated at him. Bella could be like a bloodhound on a scent, and he was tempted to tell her to do something unpleasant. He refrained, though, because he wanted his family's support, both for himself and for Tess and the baby. Pissing off Bella wouldn't be a wise move. "She's about seven months along with what just became a high-risk pregnancy and she just got out of the hospital, dammit. I need to make sure she's okay through the night. She's supposed to hire some help in the next day or so, and then I won't have to stay so close."

"So I suppose the baby is yours?" Again the temptation to tell her off was strong, but he tamped it down.

"Yep," he answered curtly. "The baby is mine. And it's a boy too. But please don't say anything to Mom and Pop yet. They deserve to hear this from me. Promise?"

Bella hesitated before answering. "I promise. But are you sure it's yours? You were gone an awfully long time this year, Nicky."

Red-hot anger swelled inside him, and his fist clenched at his side. He shouldn't be mad because his older sister was concerned for him. Families looked out for each other. But she should also believe what he told her. Families were supposed to trust each other as well, and pretty soon he'd have a family of his own—of sorts.

"I'm positive, so drop the subject and don't bring it up again."

"I'm just looking out for you, little brother." The older three Russo children were stair steps, each born a year apart. Bella had enjoyed being the baby until she was three and Nick had come along. Born eight weeks early, he commanded even more attention than the usual newborn. It hadn't escaped Nick that Tess was at the same point in her pregnancy that his mother had been when she'd given birth to him. Should the baby arrive early, perhaps his mother could provide emotional support for Tess. After all, he'd grown up to be healthy and strong.

"I can take care of myself, though I appreciate your concern. Really, I do. Tess and I aren't in any sort of formal relationship, but if she says the baby is mine, it's mine. I know her well enough to believe her."

"Did you ask for DNA testing to rule out any other possibilities of who the father is?"

"What part of *trust* don't you understand, Bella? She offered to have the DNA tests done and I told her she didn't have to do it. It's an unnecessary expense on top of everything else."

"People lie." Nick noted an odd tone in her voice but dismissed it. "Don't say I didn't warn you if this baby is born with carrot-red hair and freckles, which are nowhere to be found on the Russo family tree."

Now he was really pissed. "Good-bye, Bella." Nick cut the connection and placed the cell phone beside him.

The front door swung open and Tess stepped out, her white robe barely covering her swollen belly and her feet encased in pink fleece slippers.

"You're supposed to be resting and taking it easy," he said, grabbing his phone and pushing himself off the swing in one smooth motion. "And you shouldn't be going up and down the stairs by yourself. Why didn't you get me to help you?"

"I called out and you weren't there. I needed some juice so I got it myself. I'm not paralyzed. And I've been going up and down those stairs alone for months now."

"You weren't on doctor-ordered bed rest then either. What if you'd fallen down the stairs? What if you slipped in the hallway? Are those bedroom shoes safe on the kitchen tile? What if—"

"What if you stop being such a damn worrywart," she snapped. She stepped back into the house and headed toward the kitchen with Nick following close behind.

"Sit," he said, pointing to the closest chair. "I'll get your juice."

"Geez, Nick. Do you honestly think I'd do anything deliberately to hurt this baby?" She lowered herself into the chair with a low grunt. "Believe me when I tell you I've learned my lesson after what happened yesterday, and tomorrow I've arranged interviews with two women so I can have someone to come in and help me." Her face darkened with a frown.

"What's wrong? Are you in pain?" Nick was at her side in two strides.

She pinned him with a look that screamed *back off.* "No, but I need help aside from what a home aide can provide. I'm going to need a painter too. I don't have the furniture and decorations for the baby's nursery finished yet."

"Well, I told you I'd assemble the chest. I took a peek at it a little bit ago and it shouldn't take long. And my dad is a retired painting contractor, so I'm sure he can find you someone who'll do the job for a good price," he said.

She shook her head in protest, then stopped and nodded instead. "That would be nice. Thank you. I guess I'd better learn to be a little more willing to accept help, huh?"

"And I need to stop hovering." Because he had been born prematurely, Nick's mother had been a helicopter mom before the term even existed. He often believed that had been part of the reason he was driven to travel the world and not put down roots. Looking at him now, no one would suspect he had been a three-pound baby who practically had *Fragile! Handle with Care* embroidered on his bibs. Mama Russo had handled him with kid gloves to the point where he had become an adrenaline junkie to prove to the world—and to his mother—he was unbreakable.

"Let's get you back upstairs," he said, trying not to sound dictatorial. Tess might need handling with care, but he had to be diplomatic about it. "It'll be dark soon. Do you need anything besides juice? Something to eat maybe? It's been a while since you had lunch."

After a turkey sandwich, pickles and a bowl of frozen yogurt, Tess settled in for the night with a new romance novel, which surprised the hell out of him. He'd have guessed she preferred crime novels or legal thrillers. But then their discussions had never leaned much toward reading matter, unless it was an article in some magazine about a new and exciting way to enhance your sex life or a review of a great new downtown restaurant.

Nick had made sure everything she needed was within easy reach—the TV remote, a glass of water and a flashlight so she could navigate to the bathroom alone in the dark. He made a mental note to ask his dad to buy some nightlights when he went to pick up Tess's car.

Nick unpacked his overnight bag and staked out the guest bedroom and bathroom as his territory, at least until Tess found household help to take his place.

When his phone rang at nine o'clock and he saw his mother's name on the display, he opted to ignore the call. He didn't want to explain Tess and the baby over the phone, and waiting until at least tomorrow to face his mom gave him plenty of time to figure out just exactly what he was going to say about the situation.

Guess what, Grandma? You're finally going to get a grandchild from me.

Carol Russo, in his dad's words, was a tough broad. But Nick knew telling her about Tess would be awkward and embarrassing. And he knew she wouldn't let him off easy, either. That was not her way, and the family knew it. His mother ran a tight ship; she'd had to with a husband and four children. Even though he was an adult, he still felt an obligation to follow her rules when he was home and practically living under her roof. And after his experience with his college girlfriend, he wasn't quite sure what his mother's reaction might be. At least this outcome would be more positive.

He hoped.

Chapter Five

Nick left Tess in the den after escorting the last home care candidate out of the house. He had tucked Tess's cell phone into her robe pocket after programming his number into speed dial. A collection of chick flicks filled her Netflix queue, and the remote sat on a tray table beside the sofa along with enough water and healthy snacks to last all afternoon. He had all but made her sign an oath in blood that she wouldn't attempt the stairs or venture outside while he was gone, but he wouldn't put it past her to use her iPad to research legal ways to skirt the oath she'd taken.

Tess had not found either of the two women she had interviewed acceptable. Nowhere close. She had been specific with her needs and requirements, yet both of the applicants fell quite short in one area or another. One woman didn't know how to cook. Another had such bad arthritis she could barely walk into the house and definitely wouldn't be able to climb the stairs to the master bedroom.

Tess had telephoned a second agency for another set of referrals, but it could be another week or more before she could complete all the interviews they had scheduled. Nick would have to stay on for a few additional days. Days that might provide more information about the last seven months. Or days spent in the company of a woman in the throes of a hormonal nightmare she seemed to enjoy inflicting on him.

He could tough it out a few more days. Couldn't he?

A trip to the carriage house would serve a dual purpose. He could get more clothes from his apartment and speak with his parents to make sure they had the facts. His mother had hounded him for the past few years about settling down, marrying and giving her more grandchildren. She had three already, and Bella was engaged but no date had been set. Though she was in her early forties, women Bella's age were giving birth more frequently, so he had hoped that marriage might stop some of the nagging aimed at him.

He really suspected his mother's secret agenda was to get him to settle down and take a job that kept him closer to Atlanta. And while he enjoyed the city, there was still a lot of the world he had yet to visit. Working for *Earth Events* was the perfect way to mark those spots off his bucket list of destinations yet to visit.

Now he could tell her he was giving her another grandchild—a grandson to be exact. But just how involved would Tess allow his family to be? That unanswered question and many more plagued him. He knew his mother would be devastated to know she had a grandchild nearby and not be able to hold him and watch him grow.

He visited his apartment first, packing enough jeans, shirts, underwear and socks to last for several more days. He grabbed his laptop and a couple of books. Then as an afterthought, he rummaged through a box stowed in the back of a closet and found a pair of pajamas with the tags still attached. He shoved them into the duffel bag with the rest of his things. He had slept in his boxers last night even though he preferred sleeping nude. Circumstances were different now between him and Tess. The pajamas might keep matters in proper perspective while he figured out exactly where he stood in the scheme of her life and the baby's too.

Then he ventured to the main house and stepped into the kitchen to face the music, so to speak.

Carol Russo stood five foot ten, with a short cap of gray hair and vivid blue eyes. Her trim figure and lack of wrinkles belied her age though she had no qualms about admitting to every one of her sixty-five years. She wore dark-wash jeans, a green t-shirt proclaiming how good life was and neon running shoes so bright they would light up Times Square.

She stood at the granite-topped kitchen island, an electric kettle spewing steam for the pot of tea she felt was required for any serious discussion.

"Come on in, Nick. Tea will be ready in a bit and I made your favorites—oatmeal raisin, chocolate chip and peanut butter cookies."

Three kinds of cookies? Mom was pulling out the big guns. Had Bella snitched after all?

Nick had long ago given up on not being treated as the baby of the family. He tolerated his mother's silly posts of childhood photos on Facebook and for the most part he just played along. Now, though, he might have to take a stand regarding Tess and the baby. He hoped Tess would allow his family to be part of the child's life, but if not, his mother would have to understand and back away.

He strode to the dark oak farmhouse table that dominated one end of the kitchen. The yellow walls kept the room bright and cheerful and contrasted with the table. Bright curtains hung at all the windows, all handmade by his mother, as were most of the curtains throughout the house and his apartment. Every Russo child's Halloween costumes had been a Mom Original, and she had even sewed prom dresses for Angie and Bella.

Nick had often encouraged her to sew for the public and had even offered to help her set up a website to advertise, but she'd refused his offer. She said if she did it for money, sewing wouldn't be fun anymore. He had argued that if he had felt the same way about photography, he'd be a homeless bum living under a bridge somewhere. He had failed to convince her.

Carol Russo had never worked much outside the home. She had helped out with clerical and telephone duties at her husband Ben's painting business from time to time, but most of her marriage had been spent at home around the people and place she loved most.

Nick settled into the chair closest to the door and pushed a placemat around aimlessly. Somehow his mother still had the power to make him feel like a guilty teenager who'd broken his curfew or wrecked the car on a Friday night date.

Or gotten a girl pregnant.

Carol set a plate of cookies in front of him, turned to the stove then returned with a tray containing two cups and spoons, a steaming pot of tea, a bowl of raw sugar and a small pitcher of milk. Pouring the cups full, she sat across from him.

She added milk and sugar to her tea and stirred. "I tried to call you last night and this morning. Is your cell phone broken?"

Nick sighed and poured milk in his cup. His mom wasted no time getting straight to the point. He supposed with four children she hadn't had lots of time to spend tiptoeing around issues. "I know you called. I…I just wasn't quite ready to talk yet."

"Are you ready now?" she inquired. "Or just hungry for homemade cookies?"

"Both, actually," Nick said, taking a large bite from one of the sweet treats. "Did Bella tell you anything?"

"No. I haven't talked to your sister since the day before yesterday. Does she know what's going on?" Carol sipped her tea and stared pointedly over the edge of the cup at her son.

Score one for Bella.

"She knows a little bit, but I asked her not to tell you—"

"You know I don't like secrets, Nicholas."

Oh, he was in trouble now. But what could she do? He was an adult who paid his own way. She could kick him out of the carriage house, but that wouldn't be a financial hardship for him. The worst she could do was to be disappointed in him. Nick didn't want to be the Russo kid who was a disgrace to the family.

"And that's why I'm here today, Mom. I came to tell you everything so there won't be any more secrets. I thought you deserved to hear it from me instead of some half-truth version through the grapevine. I just had to make sure I had all of the facts so I could share them with you."

"Well, whatever's going on, at least this girl is having the baby. And I'm presuming since you're here to talk to me that you are the baby's father."

Nick nodded, a bite of cookie sticking in his throat at the thought of having fathered another child. He took a swallow of tea to wash the dryness away. At least his mother hadn't questioned the baby's paternity like his sister had.

"From the looks of her, she's pretty far along in her pregnancy. And you're just now telling me about it? We've talked on the phone nearly every week all year long."

To hell with sewing. His mother could have been a top-notch interrogator for the CIA. And pity the poor fool who had to sit across the table from her.

"I didn't know about it myself until two days ago," Nick confessed.

His mother raised an eyebrow and cocked her head to one side. "She looks ready to deliver and you only found out two days ago?"

"Actually, she still has about two months to go."

"Okay, but just what *is* your relationship with this woman, Nick?"

"I *thought* we were just friends. I mean, we've known each other for a couple of years, and when I was in town we'd get together to see a movie, go to a concert, have dinner…" Nick's voice trailed off. His mother might know he'd had sex with Tess, but he still wasn't comfortable verbalizing it.

"So, she was a friend with benefits?" His mother didn't beat around the bush. "Oh for heaven's sake, Nick, don't look so shocked. I might have gray hair and be on Medicare, but I am not a relic of the last century."

Heat spread up his neck and face and Nick once more felt like that teenage son who had screwed up and disappointed his parents. But he was an adult now. An adult who planned to take on responsibility for the child he had fathered. Or at least as much responsibility as Tess and his job would allow.

"So what are you planning to do about this situation?"

He shrugged. "I'm still trying to figure all that out. She never let me know she was pregnant, and I had no idea until I ran into her when I was shopping on Saturday. She wasn't feeling well and I called nine-one-one and ended up going to the emergency room with her."

His mother's face was a stony mask. Hell, if he was a parent, he wouldn't believe a story like this either.

"She's going to be okay, but the doctor told her she had to take it easy or he would put her back in the hospital. I don't know if she has any family here. We never talked much about that sort of…"

"I won't ask what you did talk about because I'd rather not hear. I guess I am that much of a relic."

Nick took a long sip from his tea cup. "I did what I thought was the right thing and I offered to stay with her until she can hire someone to help her out."

"Even though I don't understand this whole friends-with-benefits deal, I can't argue with what you're doing."

"I need to talk to Pop too and see if he can recommend a painter because her nursery needs a new coat of paint."

"Whatta ya need to ask Pop?" his father asked as he walked through the back door.

"I just need the name of a reasonably priced painter for a friend."

"Nicholas," his mother warned in the tone he had learned early on meant business.

Nick exhaled loudly then repeated an abbreviated version of the story for his father, dreading the reaction he anticipated. Ben Russo stood two inches taller than his youngest son and came from an extremely traditional Italian background.

"I know you'll do the right thing, son," Ben said, surprising Nick with his calm response. "I'd be glad to paint that room myself. It won't take long at all. After all, it's my grandchild we're talking about. Now that I've retired, I can use something else to fill my time. There are only so many hours a day a man can fish and play poker."

Nick didn't want to quell his parents' enthusiasm over the baby, but neither did he want them to believe this baby would visit every Sunday afternoon and call them Grammy and Poppa like their other grandchildren did. This was all part of the multitude of details he had yet to discuss with Tess—details they didn't have a lot of time left to cover.

"That's really generous of you to offer, Pop. I'm just not sure how comfortable Tess would be about it. I mean, this isn't your traditional family situation we have going on here. And she has an independent streak like you wouldn't believe. Let me talk with her, explain how this will help her out and I'll let you know something as soon as I can."

Ben's lips thinned into a grim smile. "Sure thing, Nick. At least I suppose we can be glad this woman isn't like that girl you were engaged to when you were in college. What was her name again? Melissa? Melinda?"

"Mellanee," Carol said, almost spitting out the name. "And I never trusted that girl. How can you trust a girl who can't even spell her name right?" His mother also came from a very traditional background, but her family roots were from the southern part of Georgia. Never mind that his former girlfriend didn't name herself. The entire subject remained a sore point with his parents.

"Yeah that's it. Mellanee," Ben repeated. "Every time I saw her name, it reminded me of melanoma."

"She not only butchered the spelling of a perfectly good southern name, she wanted no part of birthin' no babies," his mother commented, speaking the last part in an exaggerated drawl.

Mellanee might have aborted his baby without telling him, but this time the wrongdoing, if there was any, had been committed by Miss Tess in the bedroom with her killer body.

*****

Tess lay on her bed, propped up with pillows, diligently following her doctor's orders. Downstairs her new household helper worked through the list of chores Tess had left on the kitchen table.

Almost a week and a half had passed since her visit to Do-It-Yourself Depot and the unexpected reunion with Nick.

The candidates from the second agency hadn't been much better than the first group, but Tess was quickly running out of time and choices. Wendy the Wonder Maid, as she liked to call herself, had seemed the lesser of the evils. And Tess was never comfortable taking that option. Wendy's first few days had been uneventful for the most part. She had no trouble with steps, though she had seemed a bit winded after the last trip upstairs to pick up a load of dirty sheets and bath towels.

Tess had learned one disturbing fact when she had discussed the cleaning duties with Wendy. The woman used the same cleaning product for everything—a harsh disinfectant even Tess knew was not designed for wood. And Tess had a lot of wood furniture in her house, all purchased new when she moved from her apartment.

"Saves you a ton of money because if I had to buy a dozen different cleaners, I'd have to pass that cost on to you," Wendy had explained in a thick southern accent. "I ain't had no complaints yet."

Either Wendy's clients were scared to death of her or they had homes and furniture constructed solely of indestructible materials. When Tess had listed Wendy's duties, Tess had deliberately left the flat-screen TV over the fireplace and her prized cherry desk off the list. She suspected Wendy wouldn't mind since cleaning the television would require a stepladder, and that level of service appeared to be beyond what the wonder maid could manage. Tess had cited client confidentiality as a valid excuse for not cleaning the living room she used as an office, and Wendy had not batted an eye.

Tess's partners at Hightower, Leggett and Beck had been exceptionally accommodating regarding her medical leave of absence as had her clients, though a few had kicked up a fuss over changing counsel in the middle of their cases. Tess had spoken with each of them and explained the situation, and she had worked with the managing partner to match each client with an attorney she felt best qualified to take over the case.

She would make do with Wendy but continued a clandestine search for someone better. She feared if Wendy learned she was subject to replacement, she would simply walk off the job and right now Tess needed her, bad grammar, strong disinfectant cleanser and all.

"Miz Callahan."

Tess shuddered when she heard the woman's shrill voice call from the bottom of the stairwell.

Walkie-talkies. Tess added this to the list of items she planned to order online. Wendy could carry one in her uniform pocket and stop shrieking like a fishwife from the foyer. Tess had suggested Wendy just call her cell phone, which stayed with her at all times.

"Don't believe in them," the woman had announced with a sour look on her face. "You know they can cause the gas pump to explode and I've even heard the government can track everywhere you go and everything you say on one of those things. I read in a magazine about a woman who got breast cancer from carrying her cell phone in her bra strap and there was man whose brain started bleeding and he died."

Tess had started to argue with the woman since she suspected the magazine in question was a checkout aisle tabloid, but her wild unfounded conspiracy theories were so well established in her thought process it would have been a waste of breath to try to debunk them. Would she be as opposed to walkie-talkies as she was to cell phones? Tess would find out soon enough.

"Yes, Wendy?" Tess called back, wondering if maybe Kelli Anne, the twenty-two-year-old college dropout with the unreliable car and the tattooed boyfriend attached at the hip, might have been a better choice. Second guessing was a wasted effort and a mental drain. Hormones had already created havoc with her mental processes. Why invite more confusion? She was stuck with Wendy—at least for now.

Wendy appeared at the bedroom door with an unlit filter-tipped cigarette between her fingers. Tess had insisted on no smoking in the house, and she guessed from the number of times she heard the security system beep that Wendy must have at least a one pack a day habit. Her hair, pulled back into a sloppy ponytail, which hung below her shoulders, had been bleached to within a few shades of white. The pale hair accentuated her even paler complexion, and both contrasted with harsh blue eye shadow, jet-black painted-on eyebrows, clumpy black mascara and coral lipstick.

While Tess wasn't a slave to fashion, even she knew Wendy was in desperate need of a good hairdresser and some proper makeup lessons. If she had to guess, Tess would speculate Wendy was in her early to mid-thirties, but her bad bleach job and harsh makeup made her appear at least a decade older. Her uniform, if one could call it that, was in disrepair as well. The hem hung loose in the back and a safety pin held the front together where two buttons were missing.

"Miz Callahan, there's a mangy old cat at the back door pawing to get in." Wendy hugged the door frame as if she didn't have the strength to stand unaided. "Do you want me to call the people at animal control to come get it? Or I could get my sister's husband Garland to come over and trap it. He can take it to the woods and shoot it or put it in a burlap sack with rocks and drown it."

"Oh God, no," Tess exclaimed, horrified that anyone considered those actions at all appropriate. She had forgotten to tell Wendy about Alley. "She's my cat, so please don't hurt her."

"Well, I don't take care of no cats. Don't like them actually. Not at all. They're all mean as can be, hissin' and spittin' at me just like this one done." Wendy's upper lip curled in disgust.

Good grammar. Tess added that to her mental list of nanny qualifications. She needed to start interviewing applicants for that position soon too, if a nanny was still an option. She had put too many things off for too long, and now she was paying the price for it. She wouldn't let her baby suffer as a result, though. Somehow she would get it all done.

"The cat's name is Alley, and she stays outside most of the time. I found her in the alley behind my office and brought her here until I could find her a home," Tess explained. And that was yet another task that had fallen through the ever-widening cracks of Tess's life.

"She's no bother, really," Tess continued. "I leave food and water on the deck for her and fill them every morning. The bag of cat food is on the floor in the pantry. And she uses the woods out back so there's no litter box to contend with."

"Well, I didn't contract for no pet care, and like I said, I don't like cats anyway. So you'll have to find someone else to do that. If I was you, I'd get rid of it anyhow because if it gets inside, it'll suck the breath right outta your baby. You do know if a cat hears a baby cry, it thinks there's another cat in the house and will climb in the crib and try to kill the baby." Wendy pointed the unlit cigarette at Tess and sent her an all-knowing look.

The baby kicked furiously, and a foot—or was it a hand?—landed squarely against her ribcage. Tess jumped in reaction to the discomfort and rubbed one hand over the spot in a soothing motion. She wondered if her unborn son was protesting the woman's poor grammar, her belief in the urban myths about cats or her bad attitude in general. Wendy had to be out of the house before the baby arrived. Tess shuddered at what Wendy's child-rearing advice and methods might be, and she didn't want to find out.

And Tess wasn't getting rid of Alley, who was neither mangy nor old. At least not for the reasons Wendy had named. The cat rarely ventured inside, preferring to spend her days outdoors chasing squirrels and chipmunks or napping in a sunny spot on the deck. The cat never hissed or spit at her, perhaps out of appreciation for having been rescued and given a nice yard in the suburbs with nearby woods and a steady diet of top-quality cat food.

Or maybe Tess and Alley just understood each other because they had both been discarded and left to fend for themselves at a young age. Perhaps she hadn't really neglected to find a home for the stray. Maybe she had unconsciously accepted the animal as a sort of soul mate. A compadre. A comrade in arms. The cat still wouldn't let Tess hold her and barely tolerated being scratched behind the ears, one of which was notched—most likely from a fight. But she was coming around.

"Anyways, I'm done finished with everything downstairs." She shoved the cigarette into the breast pocket of her uniform. "I'll make you up some lunch, if you're ready to eat that is."

Wendy had exaggerated when she had claimed she could cook. Her breakfasts were acceptable—usually scrambled eggs or instant oatmeal.

"Oh, no. You don't have to do that today," Tess said politely. "I have a friend coming over in a bit and bringing lunch."

Thank goodness, because Tess's first encounter with Wendy's idea of lunch—a greasy fried bologna sandwich on white bread, a mound of cheese puffs and a sugary marshmallow-filled cookie—had led Tess to make sure she always either had lunch plans of some sort or something healthy to eat stashed in her room. One day she had sneaked downstairs before Wendy arrived, fixed a healthy sandwich and carried it back upstairs where she had stashed it in the nightstand drawer until Wendy took her own lunch break. Another day, she ordered a Cobb salad from a deli that delivered and lied to Wendy, telling her she had been craving it for days and couldn't fight the craving any longer.

How the woman remained employed was as big a mystery to Tess as why she put up with her. But just thinking of interviewing more candidates was exhausting. And the housekeeper was a buffer between her and Nick. As long as he thought she had household help, he wasn't living under her roof.

Today, Nick had promised to assemble the chest of drawers that had begun this whole adventure. Tess had begged him to bring her something from her favorite sandwich shop.

"Well if you're sure about that, I'll just go back downstairs and watch my TV show while I eat my lunch. Then I'll come back up here and clean the upstairs."

"That will be fine, Wendy," Tess said, dismissing the woman.

Ten minutes later the too-loud sounds of suburban angst and adulterous affairs floated upstairs. Was the woman deaf too? In the few days Wendy had worked for her, Tess had learned her viewing preferences ranged from soap operas and various television judges to wacky reality shows and infomercials.

Tess slid a set of noise-blocking headphones onto her head, closed her eyes and drowned out the racket with music designed for relaxation. When she opened her eyes again, the numbers on the digital clock on her nightstand read three-thirty. She pulled off the headphones and heard…nothing. No noisy TV. No washing machine or dryer running. Nothing.

Nick sat in the recliner in the corner of her bedroom engrossed in her childbirth book. Normally covered in various articles of clothing she shed after a long day at work or in court, the chair stayed clutter-free now that she only wore loose nightgowns and her bathrobe. The following week she would actually get to put on real clothes and visit her obstetrician's office for a check-up and ultrasound. Maybe she could even go to the drive-through at a burger place and get a chocolate shake.

How pathetic was it that her life had gone from the drama and often frenetic pace of divorce court to being excited about wearing a muumuu and getting a milkshake? Her stomach rumbled at the thought since she had slept through lunch.

"You're awake," Nick said, laying the book aside and rising to his feet. He stretched to his full six-two and flexed his shoulders, accentuating the muscles. He wasn't ripped like the men who paraded like peacocks through the gym she used to frequent. His fitness was more subtle and appealing. He had an outdoorsman's physique—muscles built by carrying equipment and hiking into remote locations and tanned skin from hours spent in the sun. Nick had told her about a time he had waited hours for the perfect shot of the sun setting over ancient ruins in Greece.

He moved to her bedside and the mattress dipped when he sat on the edge of the bed.

"Your lunch is in the fridge, but first I have some good news and some bad news," he announced. "Which do you want first?"

Oh hell, what now? Had Wendy the Wonder Maid replaced all her dishes with paper plates so she wouldn't have to wash them? Or had all her matching red KitchenAid appliances disappeared along with Wendy? Or worse yet, had Wendy followed through on her threat to have her brother-in-law Garland get rid of the cat?

"Let's go ahead and get the bad news over with." She released a resigned sigh. Her life had been nothing but bad news lately.

"Now just take a deep breath and relax. I don't want you having a repeat performance of—"

"Just tell me," she ground out through clenched teeth.

"I fired Wendy."

For a moment, Tess wondered how this could be bad given the woman's multitude of flaws and annoying behavior. But then she remembered she would have no one to help her.

"Who died and made you head of personnel? Are you crazy?" she exclaimed with irritation. "What am I going to do now? You heard the doctor as clearly as I did. I have to stay off my feet as much as possible. Granted, Wendy isn't the world's greatest home care aide."

"And that is the world's biggest understatement."

"I've been trying to look for someone else to take her place. I called a few more agencies this morning, but it will take time to do another round of interviews and what am I supposed to do in the meantime? You had no right to fire her, Nick."

"It just made good sense. The flower bed below the back deck is nearly covered in cigarette butts."

Nothing in her life made good sense anymore, but that didn't solve her dilemma. "That's because I won't let her smoke in the house."

"But does she have to litter the yard? Hasn't she ever heard of an ashtray?"

"Will you please buy one and put it on the deck and beg her to come back?"

"The woman is incompetent and lazy," Nick continued. "I came in and found her spraying your towels with freshener and tossing them in the dryer instead of washing them. She was, however, bringing her personal laundry here and using your washer and dryer. She was also drinking on the job. I found beer cans in the garbage can outside when I cleaned up the flower bed."

Tess found herself speechless. Nick's revelation took Wendy's incompetence to a new level.

"Besides, she called me Mr. Callahan."

Tess stifled a laugh, and then became serious. "So what's the good news?"

"I thought you'd never ask. I found you a great replacement." Nick's mouth curved into a wide smile.

Tess didn't like that smile. It was the sort of smile someone gave before they handed you a salt shaker with the cap unscrewed or slipped a whoopee cushion into your chair.

"Should I be worried?" Tess asked, her voice filled with apprehension.

"Not at all. This person comes highly recommended by my mother and works for much less than that bleached-blonde, nicotine-addicted, grammar-school dropout who called herself a home health aide."

"If she's so good, why does she charge less?" A worried look furrowed Tess's brow. "This doesn't sound right, Nick. Is she in the country illegally or something? Who is she?"

"She's not illegal," Nick reassured her. "As a matter of fact, she's not a she at all."

"Not a she?" He had hired a man to come into her home and work?

"It's me."

Tess opened and closed her mouth like a landed fish. "You?" she asked, irked by his gall. "What do you know about being a home health aide?"

"A hell of a lot more than the one I just fired. I told you, Tess, it made sense to let her go, and it makes sense for me to move back in until the baby arrives. I work for free, and I'll feed you decent meals and make sure you follow doctor's orders. Didn't you say you were going to get a nanny? By the time you have the baby, you'll have Mary Poppins all lined up and I'll go back to my place."

He made sense, though she'd be damned if she told him she agreed. Letting him take over for Wendy would be a *de facto* agreement, and she would have to live with that.

"We have to have some rules, though. Some boundaries."

"Like what?" Nick fixed his sights on her, a move she viewed as a challenge.

What indeed? Telling him not to walk around in his underwear? She had seen him in less than that. Leaving the toilet seat up? Putting the cap back on the toothpaste? He wouldn't share her bathroom so those were pointless.

"Well, no funny business," she finally said, boldly meeting his gaze.

He smothered a laugh and stared at her abdomen. "I think we've already done the funny business."

His disregard for the gravity of her circumstances infuriated her. "You know what I mean."

His expression sobered and he shook his head in agreement.

"I should put this in the form of a legal contract."

"If that's what you want, I'll be happy to sign it."

"Then I can sue your ass off if you breach it."

"Me? Breach an anti-funny-business contract?" He clutched his chest dramatically. "You wound me, Tess."

"I'm not going to bother though. I'd have to type it and you'd just fuss at me for working." She held out her hand. "We can shake on it. And understand that oral agreements have been held up in court."

He shook her hand and then kissed the palm. "Got it," he said, ticking off on his fingers. "Oral and funny business." The bed shook with his laughter.

"Out." She pointed to the door. "Now."

Nick pushed up from the bed and sauntered to the doorway, still laughing. He paused then looked back over his shoulder at her. He smiled at her again and waggled his eyebrows. "I believe it's going to be fun being your new chief cook and bottle washer."

Oh hell.

Chapter Six

"I'm bored." Tess's whine echoed down the hallway to the room where Nick had spread out tools to assemble the chest Tess had ordered for the baby's room. The chest that had precipitated this whole arrangement.

He set aside the instructions he'd been attempting to decipher and made his way to her room. A tray with an empty plate and bowl sat in the middle of the bed, and Tess was stretched out in the recliner. The corners of her mouth drooped and her eyes held a lifeless expression. Nick did feel sorry for her. Her regular routine and busy life had been interrupted, and he could only imagine how he would feel if he was sentenced to limited activity for an undetermined amount of time.

"Want to help me put that chest of drawers together?" He leaned against the doorframe and nodded his head in the direction of the nursery.

"First you fuss at me for doing too much, then you fire my housekeeper and take over her job. Now you want me to help you do what you fussed at me about in the first place?"

Women. Damn, he had tried so hard to understand them, but he was failing miserably. Even having grown up with two sisters, the feminine mystique remained exactly that: a deep, dark enigma that men were perhaps never destined to understand. Ever. Maybe the surprise his father had brought while Tess had napped would help her sour mood.

"You can read the instructions to me while I put the pieces together. It'll speed up the process," he explained patiently. "And it won't exert anything but your brilliant mind." A little flattery, no matter how corny, might help put him back in her good favor after firing Wendy.

Tess's expression brightened like a child being released from after-school detention and allowed full access to the school playground.

"Can you bring a chair to the nursery so I can sit?"

"I already have. I was optimistic you'd say yes to my offer."

Carefully, Nick helped her out of the recliner, held out her pink fleece robe then guided her by the elbow as she ambled to the nursery.

"After you," he said, stepping aside and crossing his fingers that his surprise was a welcome one.

She entered the room, paused and then burst into tears.

He was beside her immediately, hoping these were happy tears and not ones caused by pain.

"How…when…?" she blubbered, staring at the white rocking chair and footstool in the corner.

"I called your friend Maddie and asked about a rocking chair. She told me you'd picked one out and gave me the info on where to get it. I got Pop to pick it up and bring it by the house earlier."

"I didn't hear anything."

"We're good, huh?" Nick gave his best pulled-one-over-on-you grin, then took her by the hand and led her to the chair. "You were sleeping so soundly I'm not sure you would have heard a bomb go off in your bathroom. Why don't you sit down and give it a test run?"

Tess settled into the rocker and set it into motion. She leaned back, closed her eyes and sighed.

"This is perfect, but I'm just concerned I might not hear the baby if I'm sleeping so soundly now. I mean, I'm going to be completely exhausted from what I hear. What if I let him starve?"

"We'll get you one of those baby monitor things. The book says they work really well." He returned her amazed stare. "Don't look so surprised, Ms. Callahan. I've been reading your massive collection of baby books and it seems I have a lot of catching up to do."

A soft meow sounded from the closet and Tess turned to look.

"Alley? Who let you in?"

Nick paled. "Uh-oh. Did I goof? I'll take her back out. She doesn't like me anyway, though she should." He stared down the pewter gray cat with yellow eyes. "I feed her and give her special treats. But she still hisses and spits at me."

Nick reached to grab the cat by the scruff of her neck.

"It's okay for her to be inside. And she hisses because she was feral for a while and still doesn't trust people. She still hisses at me sometimes too. And she drove Wendy nuts."

"Yeah, she told me all about how cats suck the air out of a baby's lungs and a million other cat myths." He grabbed a long strip of paper from the packaging materials and dragged it along the carpet, hoping to lure the cat to play. "Did you know that according to Wendy, some cat litter is radioactive, so it's a good thing Alley uses the woods outside?"

Tess shook her head in dismay. "She was a nutcase, wasn't she? I can't believe she's the best I could find. Now I'm beginning to worry about finding a nanny. I'm afraid anyone I hire might turn out to be a vampire or something."

"One thing is for sure. My mother will help you out."

Tess stopped rocking abruptly. "She knows about the baby? Well, I mean she saw me that day at the carriage house, so she knows I'm pregnant. But how much does she know?"

"She knows everything," he said. "And so does my father."

"And she's still willing to help?"

The question astonished him. What grandmother wouldn't want to help? Of course, their pillow talk was never about family. She had never mentioned siblings, but he knew she had grown up around Atlanta. Surely if she had family still in the area they'd have visited her by now.

"Tess, they were a little surprised," he said. "Okay, they were a lot surprised, but they're good people and would never neglect their grandchild. I know I won't be able to be here all the time because of my job, but when I am, I intend to help as much as I can and be a positive influence on the baby. And of course I'll contribute financially."

Tess said nothing, which Nick took as a bad sign.

"Do you not want me or my parents involved?" he asked, hoping that was not the case. His newfound knowledge of impending fatherhood, while shocking him to the core, had not eliminated his sense of responsibility. Or his sense of wonder at a part of him about to enter the world. His job would keep him away much of the time, but he would help support his child. And he wanted involvement with his son when he was in Atlanta. Surely Tess wouldn't deny him access to his own flesh and blood.

Tess chewed her lower lip and Nick wondered if he was going to have to explain to his folks that they were unwelcome grandparents. They would be unhappy, but would respect Tess's wishes. He had explained to them their involvement or lack thereof was Tess's choice.

"I guess…well, I just never expected their support or involvement. I mean, look at how this whole situation played out. I didn't tell you I was pregnant. I really didn't try hard enough to get in touch with you, and then you found out by practically falling over me in a store when I was about to faint. Now you're playing nursemaid instead of being able to enjoy your vacation. I'm not sure I'd be overly fond of someone who'd treated my son like that."

"You don't have to worry about them. My father is so excited about having another grandson. Angie's girls are fashion fanatics, boy-crazy teenagers, and my brother's son is a junior in high school who stays glued to the TV watching car races. I've already had to stop my pop from buying the baby his own fishing rod and reel." Nick chuckled at the thought of a baby-sized Zebco. "And my mom? She loves children, especially grandchildren she can spoil and then send home."

Alley crept out of the closet and settled beside the rocking chair, purring like the motor of a well-tuned engine. Nick reached to scratch her behind the ears, and then swiftly pulled back his hand when he received a hiss for his efforts.

"What can I do to win over this cat? I don't like living in a house full of women who hate me. I went through that when my sisters were teenagers."

"There will be another male here in the house pretty soon." Tess splayed the fingers of both hands across her expanded abdomen. "And this one won't leave me." Her voice was nearly inaudible.

Nick's jovial attitude sobered. He wasn't sure what to make of Tess's comment. Sure, he had been absent, but it was because he had no idea she was pregnant. He had assured her he would do his best to help with the baby—physically, emotionally and financially. He opened his mouth to utter the assurance again.

Tess set the rocker back in motion. "Let's get to work, okay," she said, abruptly changing the topic of discussion. "Hand me the instructions and I'll guide you while you screw."

Nick stared at her and then laughed out loud. "God, that sounds dirty."

Tess gave him a disapproving look. "You know what I mean. Get to work."

"Yes, ma'am." He gave her a mock salute and picked up a screwdriver.

Together they made quick work of the project, and when Nick slid the assembled chest into place, Tess smiled in admiration.

"Now all I need to do is assemble the crib and changing table, paint the room—"

"You mean have someone paint it for you," Nick interrupted.

Tess rolled her eyes. "Have you not learned yet? Yes, I plan to have someone else paint the room. It's on my list to call some painting contractors."

"Done," Nick said calmly.

A look of confusion crossed Tess's face. "What do you mean by done?"

"My dad is a retired painting contractor and he said he'd do it for you."

"What are his rates?"

"The absolute best you'll find because he's going to do it for free. All it will cost you is the price of the paint. Just tell him what color you want and he'll get it at a discount and paint the room for you. If you need anything else painted I bet he'd do that too. He doesn't like to admit it, but I think he's bored being retired, so you'd be doing him and my mom a favor."

"If he's retired, how does he still get a discount?"

"My brother Tony took over the company so it's still in the family. I'll write down Pop's cell number for you and you can give him the details and set up a time for him to come over."

Tess hesitated. "I've never met your folks, Nick. I'm really uncomfortable about accepting all this from them. I'm sure they're still coming to grips with our…" She pointed her index fingers at her abdomen. "Our situation."

"So I'll arrange for them to come over and meet you, okay? And they seem to be gripping our situation pretty well from what I can tell."

Tess shifted in the chair. "I have the paint color picked out already. Can't you just tell your dad what it is?"

"Why, Tess Callahan, I do believe you're scared. Where's the woman who faced down the CEO of Melville Marketing Solutions in court with videos of him and his mistress coming out of a sleazy rent-by-the-hour hot-sheet motel?"

Her green gaze drilled into him. "She's pregnant and hormonal, not to mention she is scared to death because she's facing something that wasn't covered anywhere in the bar exam and she's not quite sure just how this case is going to end. The jury is still out on this one."

Nick stood and quickly moved in front of the rocking chair. He grasped her hands and carefully pulled her to a standing position. He wrapped his arms around her and pulled her close, inhaling the sweet smell of her. He rubbed one hand up and down her back in a soothing motion.

He took a step back but held onto her hand in a reassuring gesture. "I've always admired anyone who can admit their fears, and while we're making confessions, I'll make one too. You're not the only one scared to death. We can be scared together, okay?"

She sat back down in the rocking chair. "I can't believe you're scared. You seem to have it all together, and I'm a blubbering mess most of the time. I hate being like this." Her voice cracked with the last statement.

Nick could hear her defeated tone, and he hated that as much as she hated being confined to home and unsure of the future. One of the traits he admired was her confidence. He would simply have to make sure she understood she had a support team that would rally for her and the baby no matter what.

"I know you do. But you still have to call my dad and tell him about the paint color." He laughed and ducked as the wadded-up assembly instructions flew in his direction.

*****

Nick heard a floorboard creak and immediately sat up in bed. From the shadows in the hallway, he could tell a lamp was on in Tess's room. He had strategically placed night lights so she could see to find her way to the bathroom during the night. If she had turned the light on, this was something more than nature calling.

He waited and listened, not wanting to interfere if nothing was wrong. And he sure as hell didn't want her to think he was attempting any funny business. What kind of asshole did she take him for? None of his business would be funny while he was there. Not one bit.

Perhaps the baby was active and had awakened her. Or maybe she was restless and had decided to read until she could go back to sleep. When he heard her walk out of her room and mumble, he swung his legs over the side of the bed, but still paused, not wanting to appear overly solicitous. He understood theoretically how Tess felt, remembering how his mother had hovered over him as a child. He had grown up okay, and in his head, he understood Tess and the baby would be okay too. Theoretically. But his heart had a little harder time accepting that.

He heard her shuffle in the direction of his room. She stopped and moaned softly, then walked further. Two steps, stop, moan, three more steps, another stop, another moan. This did not sound good. Not good at all. His heart raced as he reached for his cell phone in case he needed to make another 911 call.

In four strides he was at the doorway. He cleared his throat to give her a little warning and stepped into the hallway in front of her.

"Is anything wrong?" he asked, keeping his voice low and reassuring though he was anything but calm.

Tess released a long sigh. "Nothing a good night's sleep wouldn't cure." She contorted and dug her fist into the small of her back. "Junior here is playing some combination of rugby, tennis and every event in the decathlon, and I can't get into a comfortable position even when he's still."

Nick knew exactly what to do, but it would involve getting up close and personal with Tess, and she might not be agreeable to the idea.

Go ahead and offer. All she can say is no.

"I was reading in one of your books about this and perhaps if I stretched out beside you…"

Her reaction was precisely as he expected. The damn woman seemed to always think the worst of him.

"Just because we slept together in the past does not mean I want to sleep with you now. And if you think you'd get any if I did let you in the bed with me, you're crazy. Or haven't you gotten to that part of the book yet? Did you even listen to what the doctor said about sex?" She jabbed her index finger in his direction as she fumed.

His first inclination was to do an about-face and return to the guest room. Instead he chose to explain.

"I'm beyond that part of the book," he said, working hard to keep the sarcasm from his voice. "Way beyond. And I heard every word the doctor said. If you'd listen instead of jumping to conclusions, you'd know I was going to offer to lie on top of the covers and let you lean backwards against me. It would take some of the pressure off your lower back and maybe you could get to sleep."

Then he performed the about-face and headed back toward his room. "Sorry I offended you. I'll get on back to my own bed now. Sleep tight. Don't let the bed bugs bite."

He knew he was being an ass and that she wouldn't be able to sleep tight. The woman infuriated him while simultaneously fascinating him. Both her brains and beauty had attracted him when they'd met, and even he was surprised by how quickly they'd become lovers.

"Wait," she called out. "I'm the one who should be sorry. You're just trying to help and your suggestion is actually a very good one."

Nick paused then turned slowly. He raised an eyebrow and gave her a skeptical look.

"Well, I've read the book too. I've tried all sorts of pillows but they're all too soft. Maybe what you suggested might work," she said, almost pleading.

"Let me put on a sweatshirt and some socks since I'm going to be on top of the covers and—"

"Oh that's ridiculous, Nick. It's not like we haven't seen every inch of each other stark naked. Just get under the sheet with me."

Nick's body reacted ever so slightly.

Down boy, he thought. This was no time for physical displays of attraction. He followed her to the bed and helped her settle onto her left side, then slid in behind her, letting her lean back against his body. She wriggled and twisted until she had positioned herself just right, then took a deep breath and let it hiss out between her teeth.

"Better?" he asked.

Her reply was a low, long moan of relief that sounded almost like her low, long moan of release when they made love.

Nick closed his eyes and steadied his breathing like he did when he had to be motionless for the perfect shot. He brought forth mental pictures of some of the disasters he'd photographed—dead bodies after a fire had ravaged a clinic in a remote area of India, starving children during a famine in Africa, people lined up to scoop filthy water from rain-filled puddles. Anything to stop his body's reaction to Tess.

He concentrated on the task at hand, keeping Tess safe and comfortable. Soon, her breathing evened out and she began to snore softly. Her body relaxed even more against him, and she wriggled again, pressing her ass against the parts of his body he was so desperately trying to keep under control.

This time, nothing helped and an erection was in the works before Tess had taken a dozen more breaths. He wiggled backward too, angling his lower body away from her.

Then a rogue thought took hold and he went from mildly aroused to rock hard in moments. What did Tess's naked body look like now? Were her breasts even fuller than before? Her nipples dark and larger in diameter? Did she have stretch marks or was her abdomen still as smooth and flawless as the last time he'd kissed his way down it heading toward glory? He had wondered if she planned to breastfeed, but he hadn't figured out a diplomatic way to ask the question.

At the thought of their child suckling from her breast, he felt his balls tighten and knew he was past the point of no return. He had to do something or risk either embarrassing himself or angering Tess—or both.

He slipped out of bed, grabbed the long body pillow that lay against the wall and wedged it behind Tess to take his place. She shifted, and for a moment he was afraid she might wake. But she settled back into slumber with a soft grunt.

Nick hobbled back to his room and headed straight for the shower. He stripped out of his pajama pants and t-shirt, stepped into the shower stall and turned on the faucet. Icy water pelted his body, and the way his body burned for the woman down the hallway, it should have turned to steam. He remained under the frigid cascade until his muscles ached from the cold, yet his groin refused to capitulate. He twisted the faucet off and took matters into his own hands, biting his tongue to remain as silent as possible as he achieved release. Then he turned the water back on, as hot as he could tolerate, grabbed the bar of soap from the holder and worked up a thick lather. He scrubbed away the evidence of his arousal and wished he could scrub away the sense of guilt as easily.

He had his body under control now, but acting as Tess's wedge pillow had given his libido notice in no uncertain terms that he still desired the woman, no matter what shape her body was in.

He toweled off, donned clean sweatpants and a fresh t-shirt from his duffel bag and made his way downstairs to the kitchen.

Desire was one thing, but love, commitment and happily ever after were another matter entirely. Thank God he wasn't in love with Tess.

In the kitchen, he pulled a glass from the cabinet and poured himself some milk. As he rummaged through the pantry looking for a snack, a soft noise at the window caught his attention. He saw Alley perched on the sill. Perhaps it was just his imagination, but the cat seemed to have her eyes fixed on his glass. He disarmed the security system, let the cat inside.

Alley arched her back and hissed at him. Nick bared his teeth and hissed back.

"You'd better learn to like me because I'm going to be around from time to time. And when I'm not here, my mom and pop will be. Mom's a bit of a softie, but my pop's another matter." Nick pulled a saucer from the cabinet, poured in a small amount of milk from his glass and set the saucer on the floor. The cat drank greedily. "Pop won't take kindly to a cat who doesn't respect him. He was a Marine, you know."

Nick realized the absurdity of talking to this cat in the middle of the night. This was what lo–. No, he was not in love with Tess Callahan, baby or not. But he had definitely had a hard— uncomfortably hard—case of lust earlier. And he was afraid if he slipped back into bed beside her, that case of lust would reappear.

He put the glass and saucer in the dishwasher and let the cat back outside, but not before they repeated their dueling hissing match with Nick declaring himself the winner. He padded up the stairs and paused outside Tess's room. In the gentle glow of the nightlight, he watched her sleep, wondering how he would explain his middle of the night disappearance.

Hell, he'd think of some reason by morning. He returned to his room and when he awoke at dawn, he had his answer. He also had a raging morning erection.

Damn it all, the next couple of weeks were going to be hell. And he was the devil who had created the situation.

Chapter Seven

"This sure beats the cold toaster pastry Wendy served me." Tess forked another bite of scrambled eggs into her mouth, then dabbed at what had fallen onto her chest. Her pregnant belly got in the way, and the baby had chosen breakfast time for his daily calisthenics. "This is really good, by the way. I had no idea you could cook."

"We never exactly spent a lot of time in the kitchen, though there was that one time…" Nick's devilish grin and the memory of him shoving aside packages of junk food so he could sit her on the kitchen counter and then drop to his knees between her legs sent a flush of color up her neck and face. She had lots more counter space now and none of it held junk food, but they wouldn't be repeating that episode any time soon. Would they ever repeat it? Just because they had created a baby didn't necessarily mean their sex life would continue.

She steered the conversation away from sex. "Aren't you eating?"

"I ate before you woke up."

Tess was sure he'd also fed the cat and maybe even raked her leaves, cleaned the gutters and done a load of laundry. He had become a regular happy homemaker since moving in.

"You don't have to stay up here and watch me. I'll ring when I'm finished," she said, pointing to the brass dinner bell on the nightstand. A family heirloom, it had been passed to the oldest daughter in each generation. When her mother had moved to the Alzheimer's wing at Waterford Village, the bell moved to Tess's house. Nick had spotted it in her kitchen and pressed it into service. "And if you'll bring my laptop in here, I can do a little more online shopping for the baby's room."

"I don't mind staying here. I have a book and it saves me a trip up and down the stairs." He held up a copy of the latest best-selling action thriller.

Tess wasn't fooled for a bit. She had been able to hand off her caseload, and thanks to the internet and telephone, she was still available for consultations if necessary. Even though she had eliminated her work, Nick monitored her computer time, claiming she needed to rest.

"I'll bring it up after lunch. You can shop then. You need to relax and sleep."

"What is not relaxing about surfing the internet?" she asked, grumpy over having her laptop confiscated.

"It's not the act itself," he explained. "It's that you would spend all day and night doing it. And knowing you as I do, you'd probably be chatting with someone at the office about your old cases and getting all worked up about how they're being handled. And that would affect your blood pressure. Need I remind you of your doctor's threat?"

No, he didn't need to remind her. Being stuck in bed with only trips to the bathroom and the occasional excursion downstairs to watch television were reminder enough. Maybe when he allowed her to have the laptop again, she would order a TV for her bedroom. He would probably find some objection to that as well and take away the remote with his often-repeated comment that she had to follow doctor's orders and sleep as much as she could.

And that raised the question of why Nick had abandoned her in the middle of the night the week before. She was fairly confident she knew why, but was reluctant to confront him. The male ego was a fragile thing, and right now she was dependent on this particular male ego for help. So far, her search for another home helper had been fruitless, and truth be known, Nick had proved far more capable than she'd ever dreamed he could be. Apparently, being a world traveler had skill sets associated with the occupation that wasn't listed in any of the job descriptions she required of a home helper.

He cooked, he cleaned, he did odd jobs and fixed all the little things she'd been planning to get to when she had the time. Nick Russo was actually pretty handy to have around, as evidenced by the eggs and toast he'd brought her.

"I could sleep better if I had a human body pillow like I did that one night." She was fishing, and maybe he'd take the bait.

"I snore and I get restless at night sometimes, and once you got to sleep you were out so soundly I thought it would be better to just let you sleep rather than risk waking you up if I started fidgeting."

"I could get some ear plugs. And by the time I fall asleep, the only thing that wakes me is my bladder. I really don't think you're going to keep me awake."

Talk about fidgeting. Nick shifted in the chair and flipped through the pages of the paperback book.

"I haven't heard you up walking the floors lately, so you must be sleeping okay with the body pillow when I wedge it into place with a blanket."

Tess wiped her mouth with the napkin, placed the fork and knife across the plate and pushed the tray as far away as she could. She didn't want to do this, but dammit, she had to since he was intentionally dodging the issue. She sucked in a deep breath and then went for it.

"Nick, I need to have you in my bed at night," she said bluntly.

"Wouldn't that require an amendment to our oral/funny business agreement? I certainly don't want you suing my ass off."

"Oh. No. Not that way. I need you to help me get comfortable. I almost did get up and walk the hall last night because I hoped you would get up too."

"Tess…" His voice caught in his throat.

She had waded into the water now, and she might as well keep going. "I'm pretty sure of the reason you're declining my invitation. I woke up when you left that night, and when I heard the water running for twenty minutes I figured you were having a little uhm…difficulty."

"It was only fifteen minutes, but who's counting?" he stated flatly. "And yes, I was having a little difficulty because, dammit, you are the woman I used to have sex with for an entire weekend before…well, before this." He waved his hand in her direction. "I can't help how my body reacts to you. It's just the way guys are."

"And you're certainly a guy. I can only imagine how *hard* that must be for you." She spoke with barely concealed amusement.

"That's about as funny as that ice-cold shower I took. I'm not trying to avoid you, Tess. I'm just trying to salvage a little of my dignity—and yours too."

"My dignity is just fine, thank you." She paused before continuing. "Did you stop to think that you are the man I used to have sex with for entire weekends and maybe this is hard for me too?"

There, she'd said it. She had admitted that the attraction to him still existed.

"Oh." His initial reply was brief, and she wondered if he would say more. "But be that as it may, there's not a lot we can do about it, is there?"

"What did you do about it before?" Her green eyes narrowed.

Nick returned the stare without missing a beat. "I'm not on the witness stand, Tess."

"No, but you are the father of my baby and you are living in my house and I'd really like to get a decent night's sleep. So if you did what I think you did, maybe I could help you do it instead and we'd both get what we want."

Tess had dealt with some embarrassing situations in court before, but she would rather deal with a hostile witness rather than her…

What *was* Nick? Aside from being the baby's father and her past lover, what was his role going to be now? Now that she had practically prostituted herself by offering to give him a hand job if he'd just lie behind her in the bed and offer physical support for her aching back and distended belly.

Nick pushed himself out of the recliner. As he reached for the breakfast tray, he cleared his throat nervously. "I can honestly say I've never quite had an offer like this, and I'm going to have to think about it. In the meantime, you need to think about what you want to wear to the Worths' anniversary party this afternoon. The invitation said it was casual dress and it's a little cool outside so consider that when you pick out your clothes."

He lifted the tray and left without another word.

He'd have to think about it? Damn. Tess wished she could take back every word she had just said to him. Her inner bitch had taken over and gotten the best of her, and now she wasn't sure she could rectify the situation. Nick's tone had been decidedly chilly— probably as chilly as the shower he had admitted taking.

And now she was going to have to spend the afternoon with the man and his arctic attitude, and she had no one to blame but herself.

*****

"I do not need a wheelchair, Nick," Tess insisted. "I am perfectly capable of walking under my own power."

"And you're also perfectly capable of ignoring the doctor's orders and overdoing it. So you either use the wheelchair I rented for the day or you stay home and miss your friends' anniversary party. It's your choice." Nick crossed his arms over his broad chest and stubbornly stood his ground. His frame filled the bathroom doorway behind her and their gazes met in the mirror.

Damn him. She could manipulate stubborn men mercilessly in the courtroom, but Nick was proving to be a bigger challenge. Her head told her he was simply doing what was best for her and the baby, but her heart still held on to her independence, and she would be damned if she let any man take that away from her. She had watched her mother's life change dramatically when her husband had walked out, leaving her and Tess for a much younger woman. Pauline Callahan had married for life; marriage and family had replaced her career as a registered nurse after a surprise pregnancy at age forty, and then one day it was all gone.

"Thinking about your options?" Nick asked, interrupting her thoughts.

"Can we compromise? Can you at least let me walk through the front door at the party under my own steam and then I promise I'll sit in the damned wheelchair."

"That's reasonable enough, so I think we can accommodate that request. Do you need any help getting dressed?" Once again, he had stood guard outside the bathroom while she had showered and washed her hair. He had moved a chair to the vanity area so she could sit and fix her hair and makeup.

"I can manage." Tess knew she was behaving like a petulant child, but the whole situation frustrated her. She couldn't work. She couldn't finish the baby's nursery. If her doctor even knew she was going to the party today, he'd probably chastise her soundly and then chain her to a hospital bed under round-the-clock surveillance.

The atmosphere in the house had been like a sub-zero day in February all day, and she knew she was at fault. She also knew she needed to warm things up, not because she was so dependent on Nick, but because it was simply the right thing to do.

She pushed to a standing position and swiveled to face him. "Nick, thank you for even thinking about the wheelchair. I'm being silly and stubborn and…and…"

"If you think I'm filling in the blank, you're nuts. I'm already in enough hot water with you and I'm not about to endanger myself even more."

"And I'm trying to apologize, which isn't something that's easy for me to do. I would appreciate it if you'd help me put on the tent Omar made for me. And I'll need help getting down the stairs and into your car. If I start acting like a bitch again, please tell me because I want us to stop fighting and be friends again."

"We never stopped being friends," he said softly. Nick was beside her in two strides and gathered her into his arms. "We only hit a bump in the road. I'm sorry too. I'm in uncharted waters here, and I'm afraid I'll do something wrong or not do something I should and you and the baby will suffer for it."

He dropped a soft kiss on the top of her head.

"We're both in those uncharted waters, but I think if we hang onto each other we might just float to shore." Tess gave him a gentle hug. "And about this morning? I want to—"

"Forgotten already," he replied. "And I'll never stop being your friend, no matter how bitchy you get. Stand up and I'll help you with the tent. Owww."

Tess punched him on general principle. She wanted to pursue the subject of their friendship—or whatever it was—further, but not now. Not when they had to leave for an important celebration. Perhaps tonight she could convince Nick to come back to her bed. And maybe by then, she could face up to the fact she cared for him more than she admitted.

*****

Nick helped Tess down the few stairs leading to the garage. The delivery man from the medical equipment company had stowed the wheelchair in the rear of the Range Rover. Once Nick had her safely buckled in, they were on their way, her first time outside the house in the two weeks since she'd bumped into him at Do-It-Yourself Depot and they had ended up as unlikely house mates.

The party was being held at Primrose Cottage where Maddie and Jack Worth had exchanged their wedding vows four years before. The affair was small, with only close friends and family in attendance, including the Worths' daughters, Lily and Grace.

The main room was decorated with bouquets of fall flowers, and a buffet table featured finger foods of all varieties and a sheet cake decorated with rosettes.

Tess made her grand entrance on foot and was greeted with smiles and hugs by her friends, none of whom Nick knew. Then Nick swooped in with the rolling chair, explaining her *condition*, and helped her with the footrests.

"You're dead meat when we get back home," she mumbled in his direction, plastering a fake smile on her face.

"And here I thought we had just decided to be friends again." He patted her on the shoulder solicitously and pushed her toward the buffet table. "Hungry?" He grabbed a plate and sent her a questioning look. "I realize you're eating for two, but I'd avoid those bacon-wrapped jalapenos if I were you." He reached for something that appeared to be made of spinach, popped it into his mouth and chewed. "I'd avoid these too. You'd definitely be awake tonight but not because of your back. The caterer was quite heavy-handed with the cayenne pepper."

Tess started to eat one to spite him but reconsidered, remembering the sleepless night filled with indigestion when she had consumed her favorite Indian food a month or so earlier.

"Actually, I'm not."

"Not hungry?" he asked. "Or not going to eat the spinach thingies?"

Just then the guests of honor walked over and introduced themselves to Nick. Maddie bent and gave Tess a hug then turned to Nick. "I'm going to steal Tess for a little bit so she and I can visit. You two can get acquainted." She kissed her husband on the cheek. "Just don't bore him to tears with a nonstop litany about baseball, Jack."

"You're a Braves fan?" Nick asked, his eyes lighting up.

"Die-hard season-ticket holder," Maddie answered. "Both our girls had Braves Onesies when they were born."

"Then you're just the man I need to talk to." Nick clapped Jack on the shoulder. "I haven't been to a game in way too long. Bring me up to date on the roster. Who's hot and who's not."

Maddie grasped the wheelchair grips and pushed Tess into a far corner while Jack and Nick grazed down the buffet line.

"You look good, Tess." Maddie pulled up a chair and sat in front of her.

"For a wheelchair-bound woman wearing the equivalent of a bedspread."

85

"Stop with the self-deprecation. All women look like they're wearing bedspreads at this stage of pregnancy. And you really do look good, especially after that little scare you gave us. You're obviously taking it easy." Maddie nudged the wheelchair with her foot.

Tess rolled her eyes. "The wheelchair was his idea, not mine. I bargained with him to let me walk in under my own steam. I do have a little bit of dignity left."

Maddie laughed. "I hate to tell you, but you'll lose that in the delivery room. It's all worth it, though. Every bit of the morning sickness, the backaches, the swollen ankles, no sex. Once you have that sweet baby in your arms, you'll forget about everything that happened the past nine months."

Maddie's comment about sex—or lack of it—brought back thoughts of the discussion she and Nick needed to continue once they were back home. But for now, Tess only wanted to visit with her friend and enjoy the party.

"You look good too, Mads. Motherhood and marriage obviously agree with you. I can't believe how big Lily is."

Tess glanced across the room where Jack's office manager, Millie, was playing a role she adored: surrogate grandmother to her boss's two daughters.

"I've been meaning to call you and explain," Tess began, "but it's been a little complicated and…"

"You don't need to explain anything to me, sweetie. I understand completely how life can change in a heartbeat. You were right there when Jack offered to be my sperm donor and you were the one who warned me the new judge might not be fond of single mothers representing children in court. That's why Jack offered to marry me. And I can't imagine my life without him now."

"But I *want* to explain, especially since I'm such an obvious contradiction to everything I've preached. I swore I'd never have children and here I am pregnant. I swore I'd never get seriously involved with a man and well, we're not seriously involved but we have gone beyond the friends-with-benefits stage."

Maddie glanced across the room to the man in question and then back at Tess. "It's pretty obvious he cares about you."

"It is? All we seem to do is bicker and fight."

"And that's probably because he's making you do what the doctor ordered, which just means he cares. It is his baby too," Maddie emphasized. "And knowing you, it's driving you crazy that you've been taken out of commission *and* have to depend on the male of the species for help."

Tess breathed out a long sigh. "One minute I am so angry about letting myself get in this situation, and the next I'm imagining picket fences and a life with Nick. I'm sure it's just hormones because Nick isn't going to hang around for long. He loves his job too much and as soon as a new assignment comes in, he'll be on the next plane to heaven only knows where."

"Don't underestimate him, Tess. He might just fool you."

Tess shook her head. "No. I don't think so."

"He's been watching you the whole time we've been over here, and I think he cares a lot more than you imagine. Has he suggested the M-word at all?"

"No." Tess's reply was swift. "He hasn't even said the L-word." The rogue idea of whether she wanted a future with Nick crept into her thoughts. Did she want love and marriage with him, or anyone for that matter? Or had her own childhood made her too wary?

She worried about sounding like a man-hater, and she wasn't. Well, maybe. She really only hated one man—her father. He had let his selfishness rule and destroy his family, leaving a devastated wife and disappointed little girl in his wake.

Working as a divorce attorney probably didn't help either. Though, to be fair, some women were real pieces of work too. Sure, sometimes she created families by way of the adoption process, but the bulk of her work was the dissolution of the bonds of matrimony.

"No?" Maddie pinned her with an inquiring gaze. "Or not yet?"

"I don't think the second part applies. This was not a planned pregnancy and definitely not planned cohabitation. Until Nick and I reconnected a few weeks ago, a baby daddy wasn't anywhere in the equation. I was going to be a single mom living in the suburbs and continue to practice law. Junior and I were going to live happily ever after." Tess patted her abdomen. "And as for marriage? Even if the word had been mentioned, I don't have time to deal with it. I'm just concentrating on getting as close to forty weeks as I can before I give birth."

Maddie leaned in toward Tess. "But this baby's daddy *is* in the equation now, and based on the way that man looks at you, I think he's feeling like a lot more than just a sperm donor."

"He is not. You're imagining things. Nick and I don't have any sort of commitment, and we're not worrying over any of the emotional issues related to this right now." The lie hung heavy in her heart because they had tiptoed around that very issue just hours before. Or at least they had tiptoed around the sexual part.

"Eventually you have to deal with it. And I'm telling you that he's someone you don't need to let get away. Would you marry him if he asked you?"

"I told you, that case is not on the docket right now. A healthy me and a healthy baby are all I'm concerned with at the moment."

"If he asked, would you marry him?" Maddie used her best courtroom voice.

"Marry Nick?" Tess choked out the words. "He's not husband material. Not remotely close."

"You said that about Jack and look at him now. He's a wonderful husband and father. You gave me a dozen reasons not to marry him."

"So I was wrong." Tess shrugged one shoulder. "I'm entitled to get some things wrong once in a while."

"And I'm so glad you were because I can't imagine life without him."

"Oh?" Tess pointed to where Jack now held three-month-old Grace. Her older sister Lily hovered at his elbow, her mouth smeared with cake icing and her hands clasping a cup of pink lemonade that she had dribbled down the front of her yellow smocked dress.

"Oh dear," Maddie sighed. "They have him wrapped around their little fingers, and I'll be up all night with Lily on a sugar high. But he'll be right there with me, and once we get settled down, we'll continue today's party." Maddie winked and a wicked grin curved her mouth. "Before we left the house Jack mentioned something about a bottle of champagne, some strawberries and a can of whipped cream."

Tess looked longingly at the happy threesome and a fleeting image of Nick and their baby zipped through her thoughts. He'd been up with her at night, he had read the pregnancy and baby books and he'd even recruited his family to help get the nursery ready for a baby they had known nothing about until it had been thrust suddenly into their lives.

But marriage? I do and 'til death do us part? The ability to take award-winning photographs, assemble furniture and be a good husband were mutually exclusive. And Tess had handled too many divorce cases where the parties had not thought the relationship through before rushing to the wedding chapel.

"Give him a chance, Tess. And you might also want to consider letting him take over my position as your childbirth coach."

"But you and I make a great team. You can't quit on me now," Tess pleaded.

"I'm not quitting. I just think Nick might be a better choice since he's in the picture now. And he deserves to be there when his child is born." Maddie stood and pushed the chair back into place. "Jack's waving at me to join him. I think it's time for the toast."

By the time the party ended, Tess was exhausted physically and emotionally. And she wasn't sure which was worse. Sleep would help the physical part, but now her mind kept replaying Maddie's comments about marriage, and she couldn't seem to get the message to stop. It was like a public service announcement on a continuous loop, and she was afraid that until she made some decisions about the topics Maddie had raised, it would play forever.

As attracted as she was to Nick, she was afraid a relationship with him would take away her independence. She valued that and had worked diligently to be self-sufficient, especially in light of what had happened to her mother. But at the same time there was another matter to consider.

Wasn't motherhood going to do that very thing to a certain degree?

Chapter Eight

"Are we going to have to go through a repeat of yesterday?" Nick glared at the woman who was supposed to be resting. Instead, she'd pulled on black maternity slacks and a loose gray and white patterned top.

"Not if you let me go visit my mother."

"You're doing too much, Tess. You were out all yesterday afternoon at Maddie and Jack's party and I'm concerned that you'll have a repeat performance of the home improvement store episode."

"And I appreciate that concern, Nick. Really I do. But I need to visit my mother because it's been a few weeks since I saw her. I'm afraid if I don't go now, while I'm still fairly ambulatory and not tied down with a newborn, I might not be able to visit for a while." She held onto the closet door frame as she slid her feet into a pair of clogs

"Why don't I just bring her here to visit? That way she'll get a nice day away from the retirement home and you'll be able to stay in bed. I'll even go to that little restaurant you enjoy and bring back a couple of those salad plates you like so much." He nodded as he spoke, hoping the motion would translate into agreement on her part.

Nick watched as Tess's demeanor morphed, and he wondered if he would get a round of tears or just a stubborn argument from her.

Tess stood her ground. "You can drive me or I can call a taxi to take me there. Either way I am going."

"Are you listening to me?" he countered. "I said I'd pick her up at the retirement place and bring her here."

"She's not in a retirement home anymore. Waterford Village is an Alzheimer's memory care facility. I had to move her there a couple months after I got pregnant. She has settled in there well and is responding somewhat to medication, but she gets very confused and agitated if you take her out of her familiar surroundings. I have to go see her, not the other way around."

"But you know what the doctor said," Nick repeated.

Tess picked up her purse and pulled out her cell phone. "Then I'll call a taxi."

Nick also remembered his last cab ride and pulled the phone from her grasp. He'd feel like a real jerk if he didn't take her to visit her mother, especially now that he was aware of the situation.

His voice softened. "I didn't know, sweetheart. I'm sorry. I'll take you on one condition."

Tess eyed him warily. "What's that?"

"That you make it a short visit. She'll understand that you need to rest, won't she?"

Tess shrugged. "I never know from visit to visit how she's going to be. The last time she didn't even recognize me, but when I talked to the nurse a little while ago, she said Mama was having a good day today."

Nick didn't know much at all about Tess's family except a few vague references to her mother, the fact she was an only child and nothing about her father.

"We can take the wheelchair—"

"No," Tess protested adamantly. "If Mama sees me in a wheelchair, she's likely to panic. And when she panics, they have to sedate her and it takes days for her to recover. I don't even know if she'll remember I told her I'm pregnant."

Tess moved to the recliner in the corner and sat. "And if you could sort of stay out of the way while I visit, then I won't have to explain who you are. It's not that I'm trying to hide you. Mama just doesn't handle change or new people and new situations very well right now."

How could he argue with her over this? He would just have to make certain she didn't do too much and somehow stay out of sight while he did it.

As they made the forty-five-minute drive to the care facility, Nick carefully questioned Tess for more information. If her mother was alone, that meant Tess was solely responsible for her, and with a baby on the way, she might need some help in the parent-tending department too.

"What's your mother's name?" he asked cautiously.

"Pauline."

"It's a pretty name."

"I was going to name the baby after her if it was a girl— Elizabeth Pauline. Actually, I'm still naming the baby after her."

Nick entertained a brief worry about "A Boy Named Sue," but then dropped it. Tess would never saddle a child with a name that would cause problems. Would she? He knew every inch of the woman's exquisite body, but he had never taken the time to learn about the real Tess Callahan. And that left him with a dreadful sense of guilt.

"How so?" he asked, curious yet cautious.

"I'm using her maiden name, Reece, as his middle name. His first name will be Michael after her father."

"I...uh...that's a great name. It goes well with Callahan," he said, hoping to confirm what last name Tess planned to use for the baby. He'd never object to her using Russo, but didn't want to pressure her. When she didn't carry the name conversation further, he filed it away for discussion at a future date—hopefully one before the baby's arrival.

Fortunately the Sunday afternoon traffic was light and they made good time to the place where Pauline Callahan lived. Waterford Village consisted of a series of one-story inter-connected brick buildings shaded by towering pines.

They were buzzed into the main building and greeted at the nurse's station by a young woman in a pale blue uniform with a Waterford Village logo monogrammed over the pocket.

"Your mother was still doing pretty well the last time I checked on her, but you know how she can sometimes go downhill after lunch. I'm glad you were able to make it today." The woman eyed Nick but said nothing to him.

"Walter is with her now," she continued. "You know he comes almost every day to visit her. And even when she doesn't recognize him, he never gets upset."

"He is such a sweetheart, isn't he?" Tess said.

Nick glanced around the area, noting the soothing photographs on the walls. Whoever had taken them had an eye for subjects that would relax the viewer. He had never given much thought to this aspect of photography, but now it literally stared him in the face. He took a few steps to one side to study a photograph of a field of wildflowers.

"Oh, forgive me," Tess said, apparently in response to his movement. "Tracey, this is my friend, Nick. He brought me since I'm not supposed to drive now. He's going to wait in the hall while I visit Mama since you know how she can be sometimes about strangers."

Nick smiled easily and raised his hand in a wave. *Friend who waits in the hall*. He wondered if that's all he would ever be. Did he even *want* to be more than the friend in the hall?

The nurse acknowledged Nick, and then reminded Tess that the resident hairdresser had scheduled Pauline for a haircut the following day and the weekly weight checks would be the day after that.

"I presume since no one has said anything that her weight is holding steady?" Tess asked.

The nurse sat at the desk and tapped at a computer keyboard. She studied the monitor for a few moments, clicking the mouse periodically. "Her weight is steady, but she's still a little too thin. The doctor would like to see her put on some weight and we've been giving her protein disguised every way we possibly can. Walter has even been bringing smoothies for them both to see if that will help."

"Thanks, Tracey. I'll talk to her, but you know how it is." A look of resigned loss filled Tess's face as she turned and walked away from the nurse's station.

Nick followed as Tess wove down a series of corridors, taking note of the generic décor and the faint smell of antiseptic. He couldn't imagine his mother in a place like this. She would never stand for the muted colors and would have scented candles burning everywhere. But if she was in an Alzheimer's facility, would she even care about colors and aromas? No wonder Tess's stress levels were off the chart. His would be too if either of his parents developed this dreaded illness. And they could. He had no crystal ball with which to see into the future.

They stopped before reaching the room at the end of the hallway. The door was ajar, and he heard a man's voice reading a poem about roads diverging in a wood.

"I won't be long," Tess said, pointing to a long, padded bench against the wall. "If you want something to drink, just go back to the front nurse's station and ask Tracey."

"I'll be fine here." Nick settled onto the narrow bench and watched Tess take a deep breath before entering her mother's room.

Moments later, an elderly man with a head of thick gray hair and a neatly trimmed gray mustache emerged. He stood a few inches shorter than Nick and ramrod straight. Dressed in gray tweed trousers, a crisp white shirt and a red cardigan sweater, he had a distinguished air about him, and the gleaming ebony cane he used added a debonair quality to his look. Nick stood as the man walked toward him and extended his hand.

"I'm Walter Hurst, a friend of Polly's. That's what Pauline's friends call her. We met when she still lived in her house in Marietta."

Nick accepted the man's handshake. "Nick Russo. Won't you have a seat?" He gestured to the bench.

"I think I will," Walter said and eased onto the bench with the help of his cane. "I had my knee operated on a few months ago and I'm still not one hundred percent with it. But that barbarian slave driver who disguises herself as a physical therapist says I'll be as good as new by next summer and can play golf again. Do you play golf, son?"

Nick shook his head and leaned against the wall opposite where the man sat.

"I didn't start until after I retired. My wife had died a couple of years earlier and I was bored to death puttering around that house. A neighbor invited me to go to the driving range with him one day." Walter shifted on the bench and massaged his knee. "I had PT this morning and it's a mite sore now. Anyway, I got such a kick out of whacking those golf balls that I decided to take me some lessons at the municipal course. I've been playing ever since. And until last year, I walked the whole eighteen holes too," he said, beaming with pride.

"My dad plays a little golf but I never got interested in it," Nick said, adding his part to the idle conversation.

"Your folks live around here?"

"Yes sir. In Stone Mountain, in the same house I grew up in. When I'm in town, I live behind the house in an apartment over the garage," he offered before wondering why he felt the need to explain his living arrangements to a total stranger. He also pondered for a moment whether the older man suspected or even knew he was the father of Tess's baby. He shook off the thought because Tess had been pretty closed-mouthed about the baby with everyone except her innermost circle of friends.

"You work around here too?"

"Yes sir. Well, sort of," Nick explained. "I work for *Earth Events* magazine as a photographer and their main offices are downtown. But the nature of the job takes me all around the world."

"Is that so?" Walter nodded thoughtfully. "Ever been to Rome?" Before Nick could answer that he'd been up close and personal with the Colosseum, Spanish Steps and parts of the Vatican, Walter continued. "I always wanted to go see those old ruins, especially after I saw that movie with the chariot races. Closest I ever got was a fishing trip on the Coosa River over near Rome, Georgia." Walter chuckled aloud and Nick laughed along. "When I get this old knee back to working right, I think I'm going to take me one of those fun cruises to the Caribbean where it's nice and warm. I just wish Polly could do something like that instead of having to stay cooped up all the time." The older man pointed his cane in the direction of the room. "I just hate to see her this way, especially the days when she doesn't remember where she's at or who anyone is."

"It must be discouraging," Nick said sympathetically.

"It sure is, especially when there's not a darned thing you can do to make it any better. I know it tears Tess up to walk in and have her own mother not recognize her. I'm not even sure Polly realizes she's about to become a grandmother."

Nick remained silent, soaking in these new details about Tess's family and friends.

"You know, I asked Polly to marry me a few years ago, and she kept on saying no. She said that she just wasn't ready to try being married again after being hurt so badly before. I gave her time, thinking that one day she'd get over the hurt and say yes and we could share our retirement years together." A wistful expression crossed the older man's face. "But I guess it's too late now."

"Do you visit her often?" Nick asked, genuinely interested now.

"Pretty much every day, just like Tess did until she had that spell and the doctor put her in bed. She called me so I wouldn't be worried when she didn't show up to visit," Walter explained. "I know how important it is for her to see her mother, but I just hope she isn't overdoing it by coming to visit now, especially since Polly isn't lucid a lot of the time."

Nick was touched at the attentiveness of a man who had been turned down repeatedly by a woman he was clearly fond of. Yet he was still quite staunchly devoted to her. This unconditional loyalty made Nick wonder if he should ask Tess to marry him before it was too late.

While he had given lots of thought to his financial responsibility, this was the first time the idea of marriage had come up. His parents' marriage had shown him the level of commitment necessary. With his work situation, would he even be there half the time if she even agreed and they *were* married? Could he be the committed husband and father Tess and the baby deserved?

Before he could comment again, Tess walked through the doorway, her shoulders slumped and her expression somber. Nick rose and took her by the elbow and led her to sit beside Walter on the bench.

"It's only been two weeks, Walter, and she's already forgotten about the baby. She said I ought to start watching my diet because I was getting way too fat. And then she wanted to know if I was growing roses. Does that make any sense to you?"

Walter smiled and pulled a thin volume from his sweater pocket. "I've been reading poetry to her and one was called *Asking for Roses* by Robert Frost. Perhaps I should stop if it's going to—"

Tess stopped him before he could complete the thought. "Please, don't stop. If whatever you do can keep her happy and talking about the good things in life, then keep on doing it. You'll never know how much I appreciate you, Walter. And I don't know how much longer I'll be able to visit before the baby comes. I hope I can come back next weekend. You know I would be here every single day if the doctor hadn't threatened to tie me to a hospital bed."

"Tess, honey, you just take care of yourself and that baby." Walter took her hand and held it between his age-spotted, arthritic ones. Then he looked up at Nick and his expression grew serious. "And you make sure she does, young man."

He knows, Nick thought. *And he wants me to be damned sure I know he does.*

Tess and Nick said their farewells to Walter and wove their way back through the complex. Tracey still manned the desk that controlled the security-locked front door, and she waved as she let them out. Before Tess could reach Nick's Range Rover, she was in tears.

Nick pulled her into a gentle embrace. Every muscle in her body seemed strained to the limit and she sobbed uncontrollably.

He knew nothing he could say would make a difference so he made shushing noises and gently rubbed her back, her shoulders, and down her arms, until the tightness began to release and the tears stopped. Once she appeared to be somewhat calmed, he helped her into the car.

Nick gave her time to collect herself before breaking the silence. "Walter seems like a pretty nice fellow."

"He is." She pulled a tissue from her pocket and dabbed at her eyes. "He's one of the really good guys, unlike my father who left my mother when I was a child."

"Have you seen your father since then?" Nick asked. He hoped the foray into Tess's childhood wasn't a wrong move.

"He popped up unexpectedly when I graduated from law school. I think he wanted to show off his new wife. I wasn't impressed, and then he had the audacity to get pissed off when I didn't invite him and his child bride to dinner after the ceremony." The condemnation and disgust were evident in her voice. "I haven't heard from him since. I did hear through the grapevine he's on wife number four now, and he's seventy-eight years old. Given how he's picked them younger each time, this one probably just graduated from nursery school," she said with a snort.

"It's too bad your mother didn't meet Walter sooner. Maybe they could have had a life together."

Tess gave him a curious look. "Walter has lived next door to my mother since I was fifteen years old. He took a job transfer and moved to Marietta when his wife was diagnosed with cancer so they could be closer to their daughter. Fran died a year after the move and from what I understand, he's been proposing to my mother for the past fifteen years. She was so angry and distrustful of men that she kept turning him down."

Wow. This revelation made Tess's avoidance of commitment even more understandable. She had watched her father leave and seen her mother's grief. Who wouldn't want to avoid the same fate? Nick's parents were still happily married after forty-five years.

"His concern for your mother is touching. And he seems genuinely concerned about you too."

"Did you tell Walter you were the baby's father?" Tess asked.

"No, but he probably doesn't think that I drive you all over Atlanta just for fun. And you heard that stern warning he gave me about looking after you. He might be old, but he's sharp as a tack, so I think he's figured out I'm the daddy."

"Do you mean to tell me you aren't enjoying ferrying Shamu all over town in your big gray whale-mobile?"

No way was he going to reply to the Shamu remark and risk life and limb—until he saw the mischievous grin on her face.

"I've never once considered you a whale, but I have heard you're one hell of a barracuda in the courtroom."

"Damn straight," she countered. "Do you know why the school of barracudas didn't eat the lawyer who fell overboard from a cruise ship?" She paused before delivering the punchline. "Professional courtesy."

The mood had shifted, and they joked for the remainder of the ride home. Nick helped Tess to her room then went back to the kitchen to get her a glass of milk. In the few minutes it took for him to return, Tess was on her side, curled around a large pillow and sound asleep. He drank the milk himself, covered her with a light quilt and eased into the recliner, his gaze trained on her sleeping form.

The subject of marriage had weighed heavily on him since his conversation with Walter earlier. The baby growing inside Tess was more than a good reason to get married, and maybe he should propose. But his globetrotting vocation was an equally good reason not to. He knew about Tess's father and how having been abandoned had affected her and her mother. He wouldn't technically be abandoning Tess and the baby, but would she view it as such? He fully intended to provide financial support, so why should a certificate of marriage be necessary anyway?

And what about the fact *Tess* had never mentioned marriage?

*****

Three days later, when a gaggle of women invaded the house for Tess's baby shower, Nick made good use of the opportunity to visit his sister. The laughing and shrieking sounds had sent him running to the Range Rover. He needed some female perspective, but from someone of his own generation. He and Bella had always been close, once she'd given up trying to send him back to the stork so she could reclaim her position as baby of the family.

When she had become engaged to Ed Wallace a year ago, their mother had only him to pester about marriage and family. Now she could stop hounding him. He parked in front of the Victorian bungalow Bella and Ed had purchased in anticipation of married life. Carol Russo hadn't been thrilled with the idea of her daughter living in sin, but the three-carat diamond on Bella's finger helped even though no wedding date had been selected yet.

Bella was the family penny pincher, which fit well with her career as a CPA. She had worked in public practice for a decade, then struck out on her own and had become successful. Her client list included millionaire business owners and wealthy Buckhead widows as well as struggling entrepreneurs much like she had once been.

Bella greeted him at the door with a look of surprise. "You look like hell," she declared.

The muscle in Nick's jaw twitched as he stepped inside, and it pissed him off that Bella could annoy him so much.

"I sleep with one eye and one ear open. That takes a toll on a man." And wouldn't that be how Tess slept after the baby arrived? Ever-vigilant and on call twenty-four hours a day?

"There's a baby shower tonight and I—"

"Say no more. Silly party games and lots of oohs and ahhs over bibs made out of washcloths." Bella gave an exaggerated shudder. "I avoid showers at all cost. I've been known to fake the flu to avoid one."

"Ever the cynic, dear sister."

"I'm not a cynic, just pragmatic."

"Aren't you worried someone will throw a baby shower for you some day?"

Bella raised one eyebrow and cocked her head to one side. "A baby shower for me? Nick, I'm forty-one years old, so I don't think there will be any babies in my future. Ed and I aren't getting married so we can have children. However, that doesn't stop our mother from believing I will give her another grandchild. At least now you've taken the focus off me after your fling with Miss Legal Eagle."

Nick opened his mouth to respond then realized the futility of it.

"I was getting ready to eat. Want to join me?"

"Just you?" he asked. "Where's Ed?"

"Another business trip to Miami."

"Again? That company sure keeps him hopping."

"Says the man who hasn't been home in seven months."

"Touché," Nick said. "You should go with him sometime and relax. Lounge on the beach and shop on Collins Avenue."

"Not my style, though Ed seems to love Miami."

Nick could understand a man's enthusiasm for his job.

"I, however, will forever love the person who invented the slow cooker," she said, ladling hearty beef stew into the bowls and setting them on the table along with thick slices of bread.

"At least you finally learned to use it. You have the largest collection of takeout menus of anyone I know."

Bella made an obscene gesture. "Be careful or I'll rescind the dinner invitation."

Nick laughed. "I take it back. Okay? Honestly, though, I suppose I'd like a slow cooker too if I was ever in one place long enough to use it." He broke off a piece of bread, dipped it into the stew and popped it in his mouth. "This is great. Reminds me of a great stew I had in the Netherlands once."

"If you hang around to watch your baby grow up, you'll have time to learn to make your own stew."

"If I do that, I'll be unemployed, and I'll be eating cat food."

"There are other photography jobs that don't require you to visit all seven continents in a year."

"I will not resort to doing wedding photography or those pictures of sleeping babies all folded up like pretzels." He pointed his spoon at his sister. "And no soccer teams or cheerleading squads either."

"But what if your kid was on one of those soccer teams or cheerleading squads? Wouldn't you want to be there to watch him or her?" Bella blew on a spoonful of stew to cool it. "Do you know if it's a boy or girl?"

Nick nodded. "It's a boy."

"Does Pop know? I mean, he loves Angie's girls and Tony's son but they're teenagers with no time for him. He'll go ape-shit crazy over another grandson."

Nick leaned an elbow on the table then rested his chin in his palm. "Everyone in the family is assuming we're all going to be a part of this baby's life, but that may not be the case. I mean, right now I'm helping out because Tess is in a jam. But once the baby gets here and Tess hires a nanny and goes back to work, I don't know what's going to happen. And I might get shoved aside sooner if she can find someone else to help her at home. It's not like we're married or anything."

"Do you want to marry her?" Bella asked pointedly.

"I don't think she wants to marry me."

"That's not what I asked, little brother. And the fact you avoided the question makes me think there's more to this than just polite concern."

Nick pushed his half-eaten dinner away, his appetite gone because of the knot in his stomach. His sister had just aimed a giant spotlight at the very issue that had dogged him for days.

Tess's father had deserted her and her mother and had left them to fend for themselves. How could Nick do the same to his child? Even though circumstances were far different and Tess was fully able to support not only herself but a child, the marriage issue still nagged at him.

Modern convention decreed marriage wasn't necessary or required. His traditional upbringing warred with modern convention though. And he wasn't sure which would, or should, win.

He stood and carried the bowl to the sink, then leaned against the counter and stared out the window at the moon, which was high and bright in the night sky.

"Tess tried to call me when she found out she was pregnant. She never left a message. I honestly didn't know about the baby until the day I was at the store getting stuff for your…getting stuff."

"Weren't you curious about why she was calling? I mean, obviously you two had slept together at least once."

"Off and on for two years," he admitted.

"Wow, that's a long time for you."

"Don't act so surprised," he ground out, irritated by her comment.

Bella held her hands out, palms outward. "I'm just stating fact. It is what it is, Nick."

And it *was* the longest time he had spent with any woman, he thought. And the longest and biggest lie too, because he'd convinced himself Tess was just a good time with no strings attached. And she had played right along, obviously because she had her own share of commitment baggage. Now he understood why.

"I can see the wheels turning in your head, Nicky. Talk to me. Don't let this eat you up like the situation with Mellanee did."

Nick placed his palms on the granite countertop and remained standing there with his back to his sister.

"After I found out Mellanee had an abortion without telling me, I swore I would never get involved with another woman. I convinced myself that Tess was just a port in the storm. When I was in town I could call her and we'd go out to eat or take in a movie or sometimes we'd just spend the whole day in bed. She didn't ask for any kind of a commitment and I sure as hell didn't offer one."

After he had arranged his face into an expressionless mask, he turned to face his sister.

"I'm hearing a big *but* here," Bella coaxed.

"I didn't plan on falling for her. The last weekend we spent together I realized I was way too fond of her and if I didn't get away, I was going to move things to the next level. You know, the one that involves rings and 'I do'."

"Oh, man, you have it bad, don't you?"

"That's why I didn't return her calls," he admitted. "I saw her number on my cell phone as a missed call, and presumed it was nothing important since she didn't leave a message. I figured I'd just ignore her and she would move on to some other guy. Since she lived downtown and I'm at Mom and Pop's way out here in East Jesus, what were the odds I'd ever see her again? I even took a couple of assignments I didn't want just so I could stay out of town."

"Like what?"

"Did you know there's a pig parade in a town in the Philippines where they dress up pigs like different characters? They parade them through town and then roast and eat them at the end of the week. I ate part of a pig that had been wearing a Superman costume all week." Nick closed his eyes and shook his head at the memory.

"Damn, you *must* be in love with her," Bella stated matter-of-factly.

"Who said anything about love?" Nick felt the muscle in his jaw twitch again.

"I know we've had our battles, but what you're describing is a man running away from love. A man so scared he's going to get hurt again that he'll eat Superpig to avoid facing the truth."

Nick shrugged and stuffed his hands in his pockets. "The pig wasn't bad once I stopped thinking about the big yellow S on his chest."

"Maybe you need to start thinking about the big yellow stripe down your back."

Nick started to argue, but again, he knew Bella was right. He was running scared and was a coward. It was time to man up and change that.

"I've been thinking about asking Tess to marry me."

"You're in love with her for sure, despite what you say. But are you going to ask because you've admitted to yourself that you love her? Or are you just going to ask because she's pregnant?"

Nick knew the right answer, but that big yellow stripe kept getting in the way.

"Nicky, there aren't any assurances in life. There are no promises. But if you love her and she loves you, then propose. Marry her. But if you're just doing it for the sake of the baby, maybe you should think about it some more. Find somebody to talk to; don't jump into marriage for the wrong reasons. I love you too much to see you do that."

Did he love Tess? Love her like his dad loved his mom? Like Bella apparently loved Ed? He certainly had feelings for her that went well beyond just friendship. Or was it just his sense of moral obligation nipping at his conscience?

"Love you too, Sis," he said, moving to the table again and leaning to plant a kiss on her cheek. "Let me help you clean up since you fed me. Then I have to head back to the hen house."

He snagged the dishtowel Bella threw at him, wadded it into a ball and lobbed it back before loading the dishwasher and giving his sister one last hug before departing.

He arrived at Tess's place in time to utter a few oohs and ahhs over the stack of baby gifts in the corner and to say good-bye to the last few shower guests.

His life had been picture perfect—a job he loved, the carriage house behind his parents' home where he could come and go on his own schedule.

Could he create a different kind of perfect with Tess and their baby? A part-time life as a father and family man? Maybe something would develop if he focused on it long enough.

Chapter Nine

"Here's to another week closer to your due date," Nick said as he placed a glass of orange juice where Tess sat at the kitchen table. She had come downstairs since Nick's father, Ben, was scheduled to paint the nursery that day. "You didn't need to get dressed. It's just my pop and he's seen a bathrobe before."

"Maybe so, but he's not going to see *me* in a bathrobe." She absentmindedly straightened the collar on her pale blue maternity top. "I might be the size of a cow, but I still have some dignity left. And since this is the first time I've met your father, I want to make a good first impression—or at least as good as a woman who is eight months pregnant with his illegitimate grandchild can make."

"Don't worry, you're going to love my pop," Nick assured her as he buttered two slices of wheat toast and added them to a plate of scrambled eggs and grits.

"But is *he* going to like *me*? I'm not sure how I'd feel in thirty-odd years if Junior here surprised me like you did your dad." She patted her abdomen and the baby shifted ever so slightly beneath her hand.

Tess had known meeting Nick's father was inevitable. Initially, she had considered rejecting Ben Russo's offer to paint the baby's room but then understood she needed to be a gracious recipient of a grandfather's gift—an incredibly difficult role for a woman who prided herself on being independent.

"What's not to like?" He kissed the top of her head as he slid the plate of food in front of her. "Eat up."

"Oh, I don't know," she began sarcastically. "Maybe that I got pregnant with their son's child and didn't tell him?"

"If my pop had a problem with it, he wouldn't have offered to paint the nursery," Nick explained. "He'd be pressing my sisters into action to do something devious. I have to be honest, though. He was upset when he first found out, but he was upset at me, not you. Then the thought of having another grandson calmed him down."

"What about your mom? How does she feel about this?" Tess asked, digging into the steaming food with her fork.

Meeting Nick's father had been her first thought upon awakening that morning. Normally, she didn't give a flip what anyone thought of her. Actually, she rather enjoyed being viewed as a badass by the opposing parties in her cases. But this? This was different. This was her son's grandfather, and she was nervous that he would think badly of her regardless of Nick's insistence to the contrary.

"She's okay too. Still a little stunned, but okay. I'm the baby of the family. She's like a mother bear protecting her cub, and I have absolutely no doubt you'll be the same way with this baby."

"Based on some of the stuff I see online, I don't think I'm going to let this one out of the house until he's ready for college. Or maybe when he's thirty."

Nick chuckled. "Good luck with that. I was sneaking out...I guess I probably shouldn't tell you that, huh? Or you'll keep him chained to his bed until he's forty."

Before Tess could respond, a knock sounded at the back door.

"That must be Pop," Nick said, moving quickly to answer the door. When he opened it, he froze and glanced back at Tess, his eyes wide with surprise.

"Is everything okay?" Tess asked anxiously since Nick blocked her view of the door.

"It will be if Nicky will stop looking like he's seen a ghost and let us in." A woman's annoyed voice filtered into the room from the deck.

"Mom? What are you doing here?" Nick's voice caught in his throat.

"Is that any way to greet your mother? Come here and give me a hug and introduce me to Tess."

Carol Russo stepped into the kitchen and enveloped her son in a motherly embrace. She kissed him lightly on the cheek then used her thumb to wipe away a trace of her lipstick.

Tess watched the exchange between mother and son, upset a bit over the woman's unplanned visit. But at the same time, she envied the relationship Nick and his mother enjoyed.

Tess would give anything for her mother to be aware of the visits they shared and of the fact she was going to be a grandmother. At least she had seen Tess succeed in her legal career before the dementia robbed her of those memories too.

"She's right over here, having breakfast," Nick said, voicing the obvious.

Tess also observed the non-verbal exchange between Nick and his father, who had followed his mother into the kitchen. They raised their eyebrows in unison, swapped grimaces and shrugged their shoulders.

Carol pushed past Nick, and with arms laden with several boxes and bags, she made her way across the kitchen. Tall and slender with stylishly short gray hair and eyes as blue as sapphires, she wore black corduroy slacks, a gray turtleneck sweater and a tweed jacket. She had a silver scarf artfully tied around her neck, creating a look that was chic but not an attempt to regain lost youth. She appeared vibrant with an effusive personality that was in direct opposition to what Pauline Callahan had been.

Carol placed the boxes and bags on the kitchen counter before sitting across the table from Tess.

"I am so glad to finally meet you." She clasped Tess's hands between her own. "I've fussed at Nicky for keeping you a secret for so long. Look at you. You're positively glowing."

A wave of heat crept up Tess's neck and colored her cheeks. Of course she was glowing—from embarrassment.

"I hope it's okay that I came today. I thought while the guys painted you and I could get acquainted, and I even brought over some of Nicky's baby things since you're having a boy."

Tess mumbled a stunned "thank you," surprised at how accepting Nick's mother seemed.

"Nicky also told me you haven't bought any bedding for the nursery yet. I don't want to butt in if you've already made any decisions, but if not, I love to sew and would like to make a crib set and curtains for the baby's room. I brought along some fabric swatches to match the paint you selected. I love what you've done with this kitchen. Did you decorate it yourself?"

Carol came up for air and Tess didn't know which question to answer first.

"Sort of. A client has a decorating business and she was so grateful for the divorce settlement I got for her that she offered her decorating services at a discount. I just told her what sort of overall look I wanted to achieve, and this is what she came up with. It's probably my favorite room in the house. Actually, it's the only room that's really been fully decorated. I never seem to have the time to do the other ones."

Oh great. Now Nick's mother would think she was also a workaholic who would hand her child off to a nanny and hire out anything else she couldn't squeeze into her day planner. And if Nick had shared anything about Wendy, his mother might even question her ability to select a nanny.

"Oh, I understand completely," Carol said. "Nicky has two older sisters and an older brother. When he decided to surprise us all and come into the world two months prematurely, it was difficult to handle it all. I had to learn to prioritize and pick my battles with my other three children. I always worried about him because he had such a precarious start in life. The NICU and all those tubes and wires; why, I nearly fainted the first time I saw him in that incubator. I was used to strapping, eight-pound babies who came home with me after a couple of days in the hospital, and here was this scrawny little three-pound boy Ben could hold in the palm of his hand."

Tess watched a look of discomfort cross Nick's face, and he shifted his weight from one foot to the other, obviously wishing his mother would stop talking about him.

"Mrs. Russo, I think you did a terrific job with *Nicky*." Tess grinned mischievously at him. "He doesn't appear to have suffered any ill effects from his early arrival."

"Well, Pop, I think you and I need to head upstairs and put a couple coats of Hilton Head Beige on some walls. Don't you?" The tone of his voice screamed *let's get the hell out of here.*

Tess almost began to plead with him to stay downstairs a while longer until she felt a little less awkward around his mother. But she knew that eventually she had to face the music, or in this case, face the mother. She might as well get it over with.

"Have fun, boys," Carol said. "And don't worry about Tess. I'll take good care of her. I even brought lunch for everyone. I'll call you when it's time to eat."

Nick's mother sewed and cooked and had raised four children. What other talents did the woman have? It wouldn't surprise Tess if she'd grown the cotton, spun the thread and woven the fabric swatches all by herself.

The men made a few trips upstairs, carrying paint, drop cloths, rolls of painter's tape and a variety of brushes and rollers. Somewhere outside, Alley hissed in protest at the ruckus of them going back and forth for their tools. Tess rose and picked up her breakfast dishes, ready to carry them to the sink.

"Let me do that. You sit back down. I remember how tiresome it was to even think about doing anything when I was so far along." Carol took the items from Tess, put them in the dishwasher along with other things from the sink, and then efficiently wiped down the kitchen while Tess looked on helplessly. For the past weeks, Nick had been taking care of her, and now his mother was doing the same. And she wasn't sure whether to feel grateful or guilty.

Decades had passed since Tess had known what it was like to have someone take care of her. That luxury ended when she was ten years old. After her father walked out, her mother had been so consumed with trying to make a living that she had not had time to sit back and relax. Tess was beginning to realize she'd done the same thing. The baby was the first concession she had ever made to anything that didn't revolve around her career, and sometimes that scared her to death.

"Let's go in there," Carol suggested, pointing to the adjacent den. "It'll probably be more comfortable for you."

Tess shuffled to the next room and eased onto the sofa, shoving a pillow behind her back for support. Carol followed with the boxes and bags she had brought with her and placed them on the floor in front of Tess. She pulled an ottoman from in front of the fireplace and sat on it, facing Tess.

"These belonged to Nicky—I mean Nick," she said, opening the top box. "I know he hates for me to call him that, but it's habit. He'll always be my baby."

Tess's hand flew instinctively to her abdomen.

"This was his christening gown. I made one for each of the children. And his great aunt Rosa knitted this darling sweater and cap from yarn she brought back from a trip to visit family in Italy."

Carol continued to pull out gowns and sleepers, booties and blankets, each with a story behind them. Tess had nothing from her childhood save for a few books and a necklace given to her by her mother when she turned thirteen.

Tess lovingly fingered each item as Carol placed them in her lap—or what was left of her lap—and she swore she could feel the baby kick a little as if pleased with the gifts that were a connection to his father.

"These are some of Nick's books and toys." His mother pulled out a well-worn copy of *The Pokey Little Puppy* and a box full of building blocks. "I thought for a long time he might be an engineer or something to do with building because he'd play with these blocks all the time." She stacked several of them atop each other. "But then he discovered cameras during his teens and well, you know the rest."

She scooped the blocks up and returned them to the box, a wistful expression on her face. Tess had to wonder how she would feel if her child was almost four decades old and living his own life—a life that took him to exotic places, often for long stretches of time.

"Now about the crib set." Carol changed the subject abruptly and began to pull fabric samples from a tote bag. "Do you have anything picked out yet?"

"I looked at the selection at the Baby Super Center and found a few things I liked. I know I don't want cutesy ducks or other barnyard animals, and I'm not particularly fond of primary colors."

Carol dug into the bag and pulled out several coordinating fabrics in dusty blues, mossy greens and beiges. "I thought these might coordinate with the paint. The stripes would be perfect for window panels and for a dust ruffle. I could take these four solids, piece them together and make a valance. And this brown and tan print would be perfect for a quilt."

Tess was speechless. Absolutely nothing she had seen at the store or online came anywhere close to what Carol had shown her. She was absolutely sure if she did find it, it would be in some trendy boutique with an equally trendy name and have an exorbitant price tag to match.

"Oh, you don't like this one." Disappointment shadowed Carol's face as she gathered the fabrics, shoved them aside and pulled more from the tote. "There's also a combination of plaids and stripes that would—"

"Actually…I really love it. It's just, well, aside from the colors being absolutely perfect, I can't believe you would take the time to do all of this. After all, until a few weeks ago you didn't even know about me and this baby, and I wouldn't blame you if you were angry with me." Tess's voice cracked on the last words and tears gathered behind her eyelids.

Carol dropped the fabrics and joined Tess on the sofa. She put her arm around the younger woman and gave her a tender hug. "I will admit at first I was a little angry you had kept such a big secret from us. But I was equally as angry with Nick as with you. Then he explained everything to us and I decided it was more productive to be happy about this than waste a lot of effort on negativity. At least you didn't do what Nick's former fiancée did. I'm so very grateful for that."

Tess's eyes widened in disbelief. A fiancée? Nick had been engaged?

Carol studied Tess's face. "You didn't know. And here I've just opened a big can of worms. I should really let Nicky tell you about it." She had reverted to his nickname.

"If he hasn't told me anything by this point, I'm not sure he ever will. But I'd like to know since she apparently did something that caused her to become a *former* fiancée."

Carol paused, uncertainty crossing her face.

"Mrs. Russo, please. Nick and I are already on uncertain ground and if there's something I need to know so I can avoid repeating some horrible mistake, don't you think I should be told about it?"

"Call me Carol, please," she began. "And it's too late for you to make the same mistake. I'm not sure Nicky…Nick could have gone through that again."

Curiosity had the best of her, but Tess would wait and let Carol say as much or as little as she chose, if she chose to say anything at all.

Carol twisted the gold wedding band on her finger then looked squarely at Tess. "When Nick was a junior in college, he met a girl from out of state—Mellanee Washburn. I don't like to judge people, but…well…she came from a questionable background. Her father was in prison for embezzlement and I was never quite sure what her mother did. I had my ideas of course, but wasn't going to do or say anything against her. Nick loved her.

"At Christmas that year he brought her home for a visit. I can't prove it was her, but several things went missing, just small things, and I think she stole them. But not long after they got back to campus after the holidays, Nick called to let us know he wanted to get his great-grandmother's ring from me so he could propose."

Carol paused, and Tess sat silently, waiting for the woman to continue. The subject was obviously an emotional one for her.

"I wondered if she was pregnant since it all happened so fast, but Nick assured me that wasn't the case. He came home one weekend to get the ring and told me he planned to take her to Jekyll Island for spring break and propose to her."

Carol fidgeted with the fabric samples, her discomfort obvious.

"He had everything planned—the ring, a hotel suite booked for them, dinner reservations at the Jekyll Island Club and then he was going to suggest driving out to the beach where he would propose to her under the stars."

"What happened next?" Tess asked, letting her cross-examination skills take over, then realizing what she had done. "I'm sorry. Just take your time."

"Nick came home unannounced halfway through spring break. He wouldn't talk to anyone. He locked himself in the apartment over the carriage house where he lives now. Back then it was a game room the boys had rigged up. I could see the hurt in his eyes, but he wouldn't talk to me. I knew it involved Mellanee somehow and figured they had just had a lover's quarrel.

"Then Tony—that's Nick's older brother—and his wife Donna came to dinner one night and I insisted Nick join the family to eat. When Tony announced that he and Donna were expecting a baby, we were thrilled. Then Nick spoke up and told us he would have had the same announcement to make except he'd discovered that Mellanee had gone to a clinic near the university and had an abortion without telling him. He hadn't even known she was pregnant."

Tess placed her hand protectively over her abdomen. Upset as she'd been over the unplanned pregnancy, she had never considered anything other than having the baby. It wasn't that she was against choice, just that she had made hers. She felt heartsick at hearing the story and could only imagine how hurt and angry the Russos must have been.

And now she understood Nick's concern for her and the baby's well-being. So many other things made sense too—his no-strings-attached attitude when they'd met, his anger when he had discovered she was pregnant. He had been raised in an environment that was all about family, and the opportunity to have a family with the woman he had loved had been stolen from him many years ago.

"So maybe you can understand why Nick behaves the way he does sometimes? One minute he's on top of the world about you and the baby and the next he's distrustful of your motives."

"Motives?" Tess asked. "What motives could I possibly have for anything?" Sure, she hadn't told him initially about the baby, but once he had learned about it, she had been nothing but straightforward.

"None that I can see, but please understand where Nick is coming from. I think Mellanee viewed us as rich, and she thought Nick would be her meal ticket to Easy Street. Then a bigger ticket and an easier street came along."

"She met someone else?"

Carol nodded. "The son of an Atlanta business owner who was a big name in society circles. She knew his family would never accept another man's baby so she just solved her *little problem,* as she called it. She only went with Nick to the beach so she could have a little fun at a nice resort before she broke up with him."

"How did he find out?"

Carol paused as if in a mental debate with herself about how much to share.

Tess placed her hand on the older woman's arm in a soothing gesture. "You don't have to tell me anything more. I can tell this is difficult for you."

A few minutes passed in silence and Tess reached for the bag of fabric, presuming the discussion of the former fiancée was over.

Carol resumed the story, her voice just above a whisper. "A few days into spring break, Nick found a receipt in his car from a clinic he knew performed abortions. The receipt was dated the same day she had borrowed his car to supposedly help a friend move to a new apartment. When he confronted her, she laughed in his face and told him he would never be rich enough to suit her." Carol paused, still visibly angry over events from years past. "That girl just wanted to ride some man's wallet, and Nick's wasn't thick enough for a comfortable trip."

A few long moments passed before she seemed to regain her composure. "I honestly believe that's why Nick has focused so hard on his career. It gives him a valid reason for not sticking around anywhere long enough to get attached to anyone or anything."

Tess mentally agreed. She had rather liked the situation too. She and Nick had a good time when he was in Atlanta, and when he left, there were no promises and no expectations.

Carol continued. "From what he told me, their confrontation got ugly. All he wanted to know was why she never told him. And she screamed at him and ranted about him being a controlling monster and how she never wanted to see him again. Nick was more than happy to oblige, but as a result, it has also kept him out of the country more often than not."

"And Mellanee walked away with your great-grandmother's ring."

Carol shrugged and gave a choked laugh. "No, she gave it back to him. Literally threw it at him. She asked him how he possibly thought any woman would consider such a trinket as a serious marriage proposal. Apparently Mr. Easy Street gave her a four-carat diamond, and great-grandmother's half-carat set in platinum filigree was no comparison in her mind. She had no appreciation for sentimental value."

Tess shook her head in disbelief. How could a woman—anyone, for that matter—be so manipulative and cruel?

"I know my showing up this morning was a little sneaky. Well, a lot sneaky, but I was afraid you might not agree to meet with me otherwise. Ben and I don't want to butt into your life, but we do want you to know that we'll be here for you and the baby whenever you need us. We'll help after you get home from the hospital, we'll babysit and we'd even like to start a college fund like we've done for our other grandchildren. It's your decision, but we hope you'll find it in your heart not to shut us out of this child's life."

For almost eight months Tess had worried how she would cope with motherhood. Aside from Maddie, who had promised to help as much as possible even though she was busy with a husband and two children of her own, Tess had believed she had virtually no support system.

She couldn't count on her mother, because Alzheimer's had stolen that possibility. Now she'd had a golden opportunity dropped into her lap. She just didn't want the Russos to think she was taking advantage of them, and neither did she want Nick to think she was trying to weasel a marriage proposal from him. In addition to her own emotional baggage, now she had the ghost of an unscrupulous woman from Nick's past to contend with.

But Carol Russo's proclamation had just offered Tess the support any expectant parent needed, and she would seem like an ungracious bitch to refuse. Plus, how cruel would *she* be to deny her son the loving comfort of his father's family?

"You and your husband will always be a part of this child's life. It's so incredibly sweet of you to do this."

"We don't want to interfere with your mother's role though. So please assure her we're not out to steal you and the baby away."

"My mother..." Tess's voice broke and gave way to tears.

Carol grabbed several tissues from a box on the end table and pressed them into Tess's hand. "I'm so, so sorry. I forgot. Nicky's going to be upset—"

"What I am going to be upset about?" Nick asked, bounding down the stairs. He had a beige paint smudge on one cheek and he'd removed his sweatshirt to reveal a white tee, which stretched tightly across his shoulders and outlined the planes of his well-defined chest.

Tess dabbed away the tears then stuffed the tissue in her pocket. "You're going to be upset that I'm dying for chocolate-iced, custard-filled doughnuts and your mother just volunteered to go to the bakery at the supermarket and get them for me."

Tess sent Carol an apologetic look, and the woman patted Tess's hand with understanding. "I remember sending Ben out in the middle of the night for a hot dog, and when he came back with it, I took one bite, felt nauseated and threw the rest away. It's part of being pregnant and these men are just going to have to learn to deal with it."

Nick eyed them both hesitantly as if he wanted to bolt back upstairs to escape.

"I'll make the doughnut run now that the men are apparently taking a break. I'll be back in a jiffy. Do you need anything else while I'm out?"

Tess shook her head. She needed nothing from the store, but she did need time to absorb this new information about Nick's past and how it played into their situation.

*****

Nick propped himself against the simple white wooden headboard of Tess's bed as she relaxed and settled against him. Eyes closed, she breathed in his clean scent as he massaged her shoulders, firmly pressing his thumbs into the tight muscles at the base of her neck.

Next his hands moved to the small of her back, where he repeated the action.

"Did I hurt you?" Nick asked in response to her soft grunt.

"In a good way. I cannot wait until I can lie on my stomach again and let Marco give me a good, deep-tissue massage."

"Marco? You get massages from a man?"

A tingle of satisfaction ran through her. Was Nick jealous? She knew she could play mind games and let him wonder just how naked she got for a massage, but Nick had been nothing but kind to her and she would feel like a rat for leading him on like that.

"Yes, but you don't have to worry about anything."

"Who says I'm worried?" he asked, sounding a little too nonchalant.

You wouldn't have asked if you weren't worried.

"Okay, so you're not worried. But just to set the record straight, Marco is a licensed professional who works in conjunction with my doctor."

Nick shifted her position so he could reach the area between her shoulder blades.

"He would lose his license if he behaved unprofessionally, so if you *were* worried, you can stop."

Nick ran his thumbs down the length of her spine, outlining it vertebra by vertebra until he reached her waist. He slid his hands forward toward her navel then paused.

"I read in one of the books that many pregnant women like having their stomachs rubbed. Do you?"

Tess had only received effleurage from one other person—Maddie. They had attended Lamaze classes together and Maddie had signed on to be Tess's labor coach. Knowing Maddie had given birth twice gave Tess confidence she would be in good hands with her friend guiding her through labor and delivery.

"Mmm-hmm," she answered, glancing down as his hands began rubbing circles through the soft, knit material of her nightgown.

Tess tapped her finger against several strands of frayed, red string tied around Nick's wrist.

"What is this? I've kept meaning to ask about it, but somehow other things always got in the way. But I want to know since those other things aren't interfering now."

Nick's hands continued their soft movement against her abdomen. "One of my assignments last year was to photograph a monastery in Tibet. One of the monks gave me this. See that?" he asked, lifting his hands and pointing to a spot on the underneath side of his wrist. "The knot? The monk told me it represents the problems in our lives. The knot is to remind me every day to work on solving the problems."

"So is my being pregnant a knot to untie—metaphorically speaking?"

"Or..." He paused and inhaled deeply, then blew the breath out between his pursed lips. "It could be a reason to tie the knot...matrimonially speaking."

After her discussion with Carol earlier that day, Nick's reference to marriage surprised her. He had done nothing but run from any sort of commitment for the past dozen and a half years.

"I have never expected you to marry me, Nick. Emotional involvement was never part of our...whatever it is we have."

"I know," he said. His tone was solemn. "But why wouldn't I marry you?"

"I have filing cabinets full of divorce case files that are damn good reasons why."

"Just because other people can't make their marriages work doesn't mean we couldn't make it work."

"Marrying for the wrong reasons is a major cause of divorce," Tess stated. "And believe me, *this* would be a wrong reason." She flattened her hand against her belly. "This was...well, it just happened. It's not a statement of undying love. It wasn't a trap to get a ring on my finger or a means of obtaining financial support from you either. You can call me a lot of things, but gold digger isn't one of them."

Tess immediately regretted the moment the words left her mouth. Nick slid from behind her, crawled off the bed and moved to the doorway. The look of hurt in his eyes was palpable.

And the ache in her soul throbbed a little more strongly. She couldn't deny it. She had fallen in love with Nick Russo and it scared the living daylights out of her. Even worse, notwithstanding those cabinets full of divorce files, she was one hundred percent head over heels in love with him. And the not-so-little piece of him growing inside her, unplanned as it had been, confirmed that fact more each day.

"Your mother told me about Mellanee this morning. I'm sorry that happened to you. I can only imagine how much it hurt you. Your mother still feels the pain."

"Well, yeah. But I moved on." He appeared to stare out one of the windows that flanked each side of her bed and refused to look her in the eye.

Was his aloof behavior an indication he would move on from her too? Hop a jet to some remote destination after the baby arrived? She wasn't looking for marriage, but she had hoped for some involvement on his part. If his mother's words were true, she could count on Carol and Ben to be part of the baby's life even if his daddy wasn't.

Count your blessings, Tess.

"Apparently your mother thinks you moved on a little too much. I'm just guessing, but I think she was concerned that she won't have any contact with this baby because there are no wedding bells in our future."

"I apologize for my mother's interference," he said brusquely. "I'll have a talk with her and—"

"Don't. I enjoyed having her visit this morning. Yeah, it was a bit awkward at first, but once we broke the ice, everything was great. She's excited about being a grandmother again." Tess steeled herself to let Nick know what she'd told his mother earlier. "I promised your mother that I would never keep the baby away from them. Your folks are great people and I'd be honored to have them in the baby's life."

"But not honored enough to get married?" His gaze shifted at that point and he sent a critical look her way.

"Let's not argue about a piece of paper, Nick. I've explained my reasons for not rushing into something for the wrong reasons. You don't need a piece of paper to make you part of this baby's life. I'm not going to shut you out. How many times do I have to tell you that before you believe it?"

"But are you going to give him my name?" he asked in a low voice. The look on his face had softened.

Before Nick had come back into the picture, the baby's last name hadn't been an issue. He was going to be Michael Reece Callahan, using her maternal grandfather's first name and her mother's maiden name. Lately she'd been thinking she should at least put Nick's last name on the birth certificate. And after all the Russos had done for her earlier in the day, she felt a bit more obliged to give the baby their name as an additional way of keeping her promise to them.

Her growing feelings of love toward Nick warred with her past and the father who had abandoned her.

She chose her words carefully and delivered them without emotion. "That's still under consideration."

And with that, Nick spun on one heel and left the room.

Chapter Ten

"You don't have to come into the exam room with me if you don't want," Tess called from the bathroom where she brushed some color onto her cheeks and then added some mascara.

She was scheduled for a three-dimensional ultrasound because of her brush with premature labor. Her compliance with the doctor's orders, aided by Nurse Nick and her own guilt over not following the doctor's earlier advice, had kept further problems at bay. Still, the doctor wanted to take a peek and confirm that all was well.

Tess hoped the baby was facing the right way and she could see his face. The earlier ultrasounds had been only two dimensional, and while it had been exciting to see the tiny life inside her, the three-dimensional procedure could provide a more accurate likeness of her baby—*if* he cooperated.

"Are you kidding?" Nick stepped to the bathroom door. "I wouldn't miss it. I want to see him too. Unless, that is, you don't want me there."

She didn't mind. She didn't mind one little bit. He could be anywhere he wanted, including her bed. He could be inside her if her bed-rest regimen hadn't also included complete sexual abstinence. Just because she was eight months pregnant didn't mean her libido had taken a vacation. Sometimes she wondered if Mother Nature was playing a horrible joke and sending it into overdrive this late in her pregnancy.

Seeing Nick come into her bedroom each morning, shirtless and carrying a breakfast tray caused her heart to skip into high gear. Just the idea of catching a glimpse of him with a bath towel slung low on his hips made her body burn with desire.

And it pissed her off to react that way.

"I just don't want you to be uncomfortable," she said, offering the best excuse she could think of.

Like she thought he would be uncomfortable seeing her bare abdomen when he'd seen every naked inch of her body time and time again. She was the one more likely to be uncomfortable.

"I think I'll be okay. Now the actual birth, that's another matter entirely."

Tess swiveled on the chair in front of her bathroom mirror and gave him an appraising look. They hadn't covered the topic of childbirth before, and she could swear Nick was turning green around the gills.

"I watched a video online," he explained, "and it's not so much the birth itself as watching the mother in so much pain."

She finished her makeup with a coat of lip gloss, stood and motioned for him to move out of her way. "And that's what epidurals are for," she replied, patting him on the cheek playfully as she walked past him and headed out of the bedroom. "We'll sign you up for one today, and trust me, you won't feel a thing."

"Very funny." He grabbed her coat from the bed and followed her, holding her by the elbow as she took the stairs to the first floor one step at a time.

"You also won't be having sore nipples and stretch marks," she said once they reached the bottom.

"I've read about some creams to help with those, and I'd be happy to volunteer to apply them for you." He shot her a mischievous smile.

The thought of his hands massaging her breasts and—
Stop.

Tess shut her eyes and willed away the erotic mental images.
Get your purse. Put on your coat. Go to the doctor's office.
"I'll handle my own nipples, thank you."

Nick's gaze dropped to her chest. "I'll bet you will." The smile morphed to a full belly laugh.

"Go ahead and laugh, mister. Make fun of the fat lady."

She reached toward the kitchen counter for her purse. Nick sidestepped and blocked her move, pulling her into his arms and brushing his lips against hers. He touched his fingertips to his mouth, his smile disappeared, but his eyes still held a glint of mischief. Tess pressed her palm against his chest to push him away; his heart pounded beneath her hand.

Just as hers had pounded at the thought of his hands on her breasts.

Stop. It. Now.

"See?" he said. "No more laughing. What if I volunteer to do the laundry by beating dirty diapers on a rock in the creek out back? Will that give me equal suffering?"

"Knowing some of the places you've traveled, I wouldn't be surprised if you hadn't actually learned that handy little trick." Tess had followed his career and knew he had travelled to every continent, most more than a few times.

She also knew he could be called away at any moment to photograph something on any one of those seven continents. That's why she needed to tamp down this desire, give her libido a stern lecture about pointless yearnings and keep her mind focused on the task at hand: to make sure she got as close to her due date as possible and give birth to a healthy baby boy.

Nick helped with her coat then held her hand as she maneuvered down the garage steps and into his Range Rover for the drive to her obstetrician's office.

"You need to show me what kind of car seat I should buy," he commented as he turned out of her subdivision and headed toward the main highway.

"There's no need for you to spend the money. If you need one, you can just borrow mine."

"But that's a lot of trouble, isn't it? Switching the seats from car to car?"

"Not really. And since your car will just stay parked at your place most of the time while you're gone, it doesn't make sense to invest money in a car seat the baby will probably have outgrown by the time you need to use it again."

"How I invest my money is my own damn business," Nick spat out.

Tess observed a muscle in his jaw tighten with anger. Now wasn't the time to fight with him, not when she was en route to the doctor's office. She didn't need her blood pressure to spike or to start having contractions, because she didn't want to be put back in the hospital.

She had been bored to tears at home, but at least she was surrounded by her belongings and occasionally got to consult by telephone on one of the cases she had passed on to a colleague. Because Nick and his father had painted the nursery several days before, she had been able to putter about a bit in the room, putting away some of the gifts she had received at her shower along with the baby things Carol had given her.

"I'll write down the names of several different good ones and you can pick the one you like best." She made a conscious effort to relax and absentmindedly rubbed her belly.

"That went well," Nick said, with a hint of sarcasm in his voice. "And it was way too easy. Are you getting soft on me, Callahan?"

Tess clenched the edge of her seat with her hand. "Not soft at all. I just… It's just not worth arguing over. If you want to buy a whole damn store full of baby things that you won't be here to use, I'm not going to waste my breath trying to talk you out of it."

"I'll be here to use it."

"Yeah, you'll be here until you get that middle of the night phone call about the next big story that has come along. And then you'll be gone again in a heartbeat, just like the night I got pregnant."

"I didn't know you got pregnant. Hell, *you* didn't know that night. It's not like we were trying or anything. And I have to make a living."

"My point exactly. You say you want to provide financially for the baby and to do that you have to go wherever the magazine sends you."

"So now I'm damned if I do, and damned if I don't? What am I supposed to do, Tess? Quit working for *Earth Events* and start photographing soccer teams and high school proms? That's not who I am. That's just taking pictures. I tell a story with images. *That* is what I do," he said emphatically. "And I do it well. And those kinds of stories don't always happen right in your backyard or mine."

"I'm not damning you at all, Nick. I'm just stating the facts and being pragmatic." Her voice quivered. "And can we please stop arguing about this now?"

"Yeah." Nick tapped the steering wheel as he waited for a line of traffic to clear so he could make a left turn.

Tess leaned back against the headrest, inhaled deeply and released the breath in a long hiss. Once, twice, three times. Nick reached over and laid his hand on her arm.

"Everything okay?"

"No." At the sound of his quick inhalation, she added, "I'm not having contractions if that's what you're asking. I'm just… I don't know what I am. Scared, tired, mad at myself." She stopped the confession, having said more than she should, revealing the vulnerability that frustrated the hell out of her. Maybe now she'd admitted it, she could move past it.

The argument was over for now, but they'd probably resume it at some point because she couldn't stop treating all this—Nick, her perceived detention, their forced proximity—as a court case to be tried and won. She'd work on that, though it went against the skills she'd honed in over a decade of litigating. Right now she needed to get through this doctor's visit with no complications and return home where she could keep marking the days off the calendar until her due date.

*****

The nurse checked Tess's weight and blood pressure then had her lay on the examination table. Nick perched on a stool beside the table, feeling like the proverbial fish out of water.

"Would you like to hear the baby's heartbeat?" the nurse asked Tess.

"I don't need to. I've heard it before."

"I haven't," Nick interjected. He leveled his gaze at Tess. "And I'd like to."

Tess gave the go-ahead. The nurse pulled up Tess's loose maternity top, slipped her slacks and underwear down and tucked a towel between the material and Tess's skin. She squirted a small amount of gel onto Tess's belly, then took a wand attached to a device resembling a walkie-talkie and ran it back and forth through the gel. A loud swishing sound filled the room.

"Is that the baby?" Nick asked.

"That's the mother's blood running through an artery in the abdomen," she explained. "You'll know the baby's heartbeat once we find it." She continued to rub the wand back and forth until a sound like a galloping horse came through the speaker. "There he is," she said and held the device steady in one spot.

"Is that normal? For it to be so fast?"

"I thought you'd read all my books," Tess quipped.

He rolled his eyes. "I must have missed that part in the thirty-something tomes in your pregnancy library. Did you come across a fire sale or something?"

"Something," she retorted.

"It's perfectly normal," the nurse assured him. "So far everything looks and sounds good for a thirty-five- to thirty-six-week pregnancy. Of course, the ultrasound might date him a week or two differently, but these dates are never exact. I always say I've never yet seen a baby born with a calendar in its hand."

The nurse wiped away the gel and covered Tess with a sheet. "That's all for me. Dr. Merrell will be in to see you shortly."

The exam room door closed, and Tess rested one hand on her belly while she slid the other one behind her head and stared at the ceiling. That's where Nick wanted to look too rather than at all the diagrams on the walls—an artist's renderings of pregnant women in profile, cut away to show the various stages of gestation. They began with the first few cells after conception and continued month by month to a fully developed fetus, head down and poised for birth and a woman with full breasts and darkened nipples.

Sure, he had read Tess's books and seen the illustrations in them, but here they were more in the context of reality, and he was both embarrassed and terrified. Except for the bared bit of abdomen while listening to the heartbeat, he had not seen Tess without some sort of clothing since the night they had conceived the baby.

The silence was palpable until Nick broke it. "Is this the first ultrasound you've had?" he asked, his voice strained.

"I've had several actually. The first one was early on to confirm the pregnancy, and I had another one at around four months when I had an amniocentesis done to rule out any genetic issues. That's when I found out I was having a boy. That was also about the time I had to put my mother in Waterford."

"That must have been really difficult for you. I'm sorry I wasn't here to help you then." One more thing she'd had to handle alone. No wonder her stress level was off the charts.

He saw her swallow. "It was one of the hardest things I've ever had to do. Mama had been living in a retirement facility for a few years because it was too much for her to keep up the house and yard. We picked it out together and even bought her a few pieces of new furniture for it. Not much, but enough to make it a new start for her. She refused to give up her bedroom suite, but I did persuade her to buy a new mattress since hers was twenty years old and sagged in the middle. Oh, the fuss she put up about that."

"It sounds like you got your stubborn streak from her," Nick said. "Not that stubborn is bad or anything. I mean, stubborn can be a good thing when you're standing up for what's right."

Tess reached out and patted him on the knee. "It's okay. I know what you mean, and I'm sorry I was so obnoxious in the car. I'm nervous about this visit and anxious in general about the baby."

"Anxious? You said in the car you were okay." A terrified sensation washed over him.

"Calm down, Nick. I'm as fine as I can be, all things considered. Pregnant women are just anxious in general. We worry. And from what I hear, it won't get any better once he's born. Then I'll be checking him every hour to make sure he's still breathing, concerned about whether he's eating too much or too little and if my milk is good enough and is he warm enough or have I put too many clothes on him."

"And that's just until he goes off to college," Nick interjected. "Then if he's like me, he'll give you a whole new set of worries and your hair can turn gray like my mother's has."

"Are you trying to scare me or just give me a heads-up eighteen years in advance?"

"Actually I'm thinking I need to zip it before my mouth gets me in trouble again."

Before Tess could reply, the door opened and the doctor walked in accompanied by a different nurse. He greeted Nick and the two men shook hands. Then the doctor washed up and moved to Tess's side. He pulled back the sheet and palpated her abdomen.

"If it's agreeable with Tess, would you like to feel the baby, Mr. Russo?" he asked. He glanced at Tess and waited until she gave her approval. "Put your hand here." He guided Nick's hand into position. "Feel that? It's the baby's buttocks."

Nick flattened his palm against Tess's skin. The medical diagrams were only a hint of reality. *This* was reality—his child, his flesh and blood right underneath his hand. He glanced from his hand to Tess's face. Four heartbeats of eye contact prompted countless emotions to flood over him, but the words to accompany them would have to wait until later.

"And here is his head way down here," the doctor continued, breaking the spell. "This is good. I like to have them head first when they're born." He pointed his index finger at her. "I want you to tell him every day to stay that way, okay?"

"I'll do my best, but you know how little boys can be sometimes." She grinned at Nick as she made the remark.

"That, I do. My wife and I have four of them—six-year-old triplets and a two-year-old singleton. They keep us on our toes for sure."

Nick started to ask how his wife coped with him being called out at all hours, but stopped short. There was no point in reminding Tess of their earlier argument. He and the doctor had both chosen their professions. No doubt the doctor's wife accepted the interrupted dinners and missed birthday parties. But births didn't last for weeks or months like some photography assignments did.

"Everything looks good here," he said, bringing the conversation back to medical matters. "Let's get you down to the ultrasound room and we'll take a good look at this little guy." The nurse helped Tess put her clothing back in place and get off the table.

"Are you going to join us?" the doctor asked, looking straight at Nick.

"Absolutely. I wouldn't miss it."

After they were situated in a different room, the ultrasound tech, a petite young woman with a pixie haircut, squeezed a blob of gel on Tess's once again bare abdomen and placed the oval-shaped thing Tess told him was a transducer against her skin. An image appeared on the screen, and after pressing several buttons on the console the tech began to move the transducer until a clear view of the baby's profile showed on the screen.

Tess reached out her hand toward Nick and he clasped it firmly, her skin warm against his.

The technician moved the transducer again, and Nick gasped when the clear image of the baby's face appeared. His eyes were closed and his tiny hand was beside his head, the long, thin fingers splayed along his cheek.

"Look at those chubby cheeks and lips," the tech commented. "It won't be long until you can kiss them." She turned back to the console, marked off an area of the display and froze the image. "Here's one for your baby book."

She returned the scan to real time and Nick watched for a few minutes more, mesmerized by the sight before him. Then, without warning, the baby smiled. "Look at him," Nick whispered, awed by the expression. It was as if his son was saying, "I'm okay and I can't wait to meet you."

"I've been doing ultrasounds for a long time, but until we started doing the three-dimensional ones, I never saw facial expressions on babies in utero. I remember the first time I saw it. I was as astonished as the parents were." The tech captured the smile in a freeze frame too. "I'm convinced if we watched an unborn baby all the time we'd see the same expressions they have once they're out of the uterus."

Dr. Merrell examined the ultrasound photos on a computer screen, compared them to other data in Tess's file and declared the baby to be perfect.

"Of course, he's perfect," Tess said with a laugh. "He's mine. How could he be anything but perfect?"

"I still want you to take it easy; my threat about putting you in the hospital still stands," the doctor warned her sternly. "And you," he said, pointing directly at Nick, "make sure she does. If we can get you another week or two along, then we can stop worrying about when he arrives. By thirty-six or thirty-seven weeks, everything is developed and the baby just puts on fat. If he comes a little early, you can fatten him up at home. You're planning to breastfeed, right?"

Tess nodded.

"Good. It's not only great for the baby, but for the mother as well. Helps you get your figure back sooner and also provides lots of health benefits. Be sure to ask for help from the lactation nurse if you need it. That's why she's there—to make sure the baby is feeding well."

Tess nodded and asked a few questions. Nick listened intently, hoping he could remember it all.

"I'll see you again in a week," the doctor said. "You'll be on a weekly office visit schedule until the baby arrives."

When they were ready to leave, the ultrasound tech gave Tess an envelope. "These are for your scrapbook."

Tess looked inside and pulled out a DVD case along with the still pictures, which looked almost like old-fashioned sepia photographs. She and Nick stood side by side and viewed them—the profile, the hand beside his face. When they reached the photo with the baby's smile, Nick sucked in a breath. He stood fixed to the spot because looking at the photo was almost like looking in a mirror, only the face staring back was decades younger.

"He looks like you." Tess's voice was the softest of whispers. "You can make a copy of the DVD when we get home and give it to your mom. I think she'd like to see her grandson."

Nick squeezed her shoulder, speechless as yet one more dose of reality struck.

Tess spoke to the receptionist to schedule her next appointment, and soon she and Nick were heading back to her house.

"Would you like to stop for lunch somewhere?" he asked when they were halfway to the house.

"Oh yes, please. I'm famished. And I would be beyond thrilled to dine somewhere other than my bedroom, den or kitchen."

"Just name the place and that's where we'll go. Your wish is my command."

*****

Nick chewed the bite of steak sandwich absentmindedly, his focus on the photos in his hand. Tess had referred to the baby as *hers* but the sweet face belonged to him. The resemblance was astonishing, and now he couldn't wait to meet his son in person. To hold him, tell him he was loved, introduce him to his Grammy and Poppa and all his aunts, uncles and cousins.

Until now, all this had been surreal—an enlarged abdomen, books on every pregnancy and child-related topic imaginable, and a room with baby clothes and an unassembled crib and changing table.

But the smiling face in the photo brought it all into focus. This was a real baby. A living, soon-to-be-breathing human that carried his DNA. And he already loved this child—this son of his—with all his heart.

This pregnancy had also rekindled all of the old memories of the baby Mellanee had aborted without his knowledge and the grief he had suffered after learning what she had done. He had never known if the baby was a boy or girl. Had never seen a face, a smile, a tiny hand. But Nick had seen this baby and felt it move. How was he ever going to be able to leave when his vacation was over?

Because he had worked steadily since March, he'd been able to shame his boss into giving him time off until after the first of the year. Maybe he could finesse a little more vacation time so he could hang around a bit longer.

"…so do you think maybe you can take me to see my mother again this weekend? It might be the last time I can go before the baby arrives."

Nick realized Tess had been talking to him the whole time he had been daydreaming, and he yanked his thoughts to the conversation at hand.

"I think that can be arranged," he said.

Tess's face brightened and she beamed like a child who had just received the special toy she had begged Santa to bring.

"*If* you rest this week like the doctor said."

She wadded a napkin and tossed it at him. "You're mean," she replied, a scowl darkening her expression.

He tossed it back. "I'm just following the doctor's orders like you should be doing to make sure Junior stays put a little while longer."

"You heard him. If I can hold on another week or two, we should be in the clear."

Nick would never wish any harm to Tess or the baby, but if he did arrive a little early, that would mean more time for Nick to get to know his son. Of course, it could also mean more time for Nick to become emotionally attached not only to the baby, but to the gorgeous woman sitting across from him.

Oh hell, who was he kidding? He was already emotionally attached to her.

Nick watched Tess practically inhale a turkey sandwich, and after she indulged in a bowl of her favorite peach cobbler with vanilla bean ice cream, Nick made quick work of getting her home and upstairs to her room.

"I don't want a nap," she said, yawning in spite of her words. "I want to do something, anything but stare at my bedroom walls."

"You're doing something." He retrieved her nightgown from the bathroom and pressed into her hands. "Something very important. You're hatching a baby. So put this on, settle down and incubate while this rooster puts the crib and changing table together."

"I want to help," she whined. "I can read the instructions and hand you the tools." She tried to hide another big yawn behind her hand.

He grasped her by the shoulders and slowly edged her backward until the backs of her legs hit the mattress. "Sit." When she complied, he removed her shoes and socks "Do you want me to undress you too?"

"It's not like you haven't had practice before," she teased.

He had. Lots of times. Lots of places. And his dick twitched at the memories. In the past a twitch was the only prompt he needed to take her to bed. Now? The twitch was a reminder of reality.

"It was a rhetorical question, really. Put your gown on and sleep," he ordered. "Don't let me come in here and find you working the crossword puzzle or gabbing on the phone."

"But I'm sick of doing nothing."

He thought for a moment. "I'll make you a deal. You take a nap while I put the crib and changing table together and when you wake up, I'll help you finish sorting through that pile of loot you received at the baby shower. Okay?"

She didn't budge.

"Okay?" He stretched out the two syllables.

"All right."

Nick let out a soft snort. "See how easy that was?"

She gave him a look that could have blistered an iron skillet. "Help me up so I can put on this couture sleepwear."

Once she'd changed, Nick situated her with an array of pillows, and by the time he covered her with a light blanket, her eyes had already drifted shut. He lifted his fingertips to his lips and then brushed them across her cheek. "Goodnight, Tessie," he whispered.

Less than a year earlier, the woman could have spent an entire weekend in bed with him with only power naps to revive her energy. Now she required daily afternoon naps, and she was usually asleep at night before the prime-time television shows began. Apparently, pregnancy was much harder work than he had ever imagined.

*****

Tess struggled to reach for the phone. The ringing had wakened her, but when she pulled it from its cradle, she realized it wasn't the landline but rather Nick's cell phone. She blinked the sleep from her eyes and pushed herself to a sitting position. She started to call out to him, but then she heard him speaking from down the hallway.

"Bulgaria? Pete, I can't go to Bulgaria right now. I told you I have a family situation here, and you promised I could stay put in Atlanta until after the first of the year."

Nick must have put the cell on speaker phone mode because she could hear the caller but she wasn't close enough to make out the specifics of the other side of the conversation.

Curiosity got the better of her, and she quietly inched off the bed and tiptoed to the doorway, hoping she could hear more.

"Nick, this is the archaeological find of the twenty-first century," the male voice on the cell phone explained. "A team from the university in Sofia has found what they think is an early Christian monastery dating from the Byzantine era. I've seen some rough photos of what they've found and it's unbelievably amazing— gold, silver and marble reliquaries, mosaics and marble revetments."

It all sounded like a foreign language to Tess, but Nick's response indicated he understood completely what was being described to him.

"Pete, the stuff's been there since the sixth century. Can't it wait a little bit longer before *Earth Events* does a feature article on it?"

"The publisher wants it done and wants it done *now*, and my boss is campaigning hard to get Jim Mercer assigned to do the shoot."

"Oh, hell," Nick said, the contempt in his voice obvious. "He might as well assign a four-year-old preschooler to take the pictures with a disposable camera. Jim Mercer doesn't have the experience or the equipment to handle a job of that caliber."

"He might not have the experience, but his mother is related to the publisher and nepotism has reared its ugly head."

"Shit. I hate crap like that."

"So do I. And once I show my boss the garbage Mercer turned in for that last job his family connections got him, you'll be a shoe-in. Relative or not, the magazine isn't going to publish anything less than the best, especially for a find like this. We have a stellar reputation to maintain, Nick, and you're part of why that reputation is so good."

"I don't know, Pete," Nick began.

"Listen, a final decision isn't going to come down until the early part of next week. Surely you can solve your family situation by then, can't you? I mean, when has Nick Russo ever turned down the chance for a big scoop? Especially the scoop of the year?"

Never.

Tess knew that from experience. More than once, a planned weekend together had been cut short because Nick got a phone call telling him to fly to some exotic locale on a moment's notice. The last time had been the night she had conceived. The fact Nick hadn't refused outright showed that he would consider putting his job first over her and the baby.

Why had she allowed her emotions to cloud the situation? Why did she expect anything different to happen? She returned to her bed, a heartsick sensation sweeping over her.

Any hope she'd had of Nick sticking around had turned to ashes after hearing that phone call.

She had been foolish to believe Nick would settle down. Her child was going to grow up without a father just like she had. She had at least had ten years with her father living in the house with her and her mother. Her child might not have even that.

Chapter Eleven

Tess relaxed into the rocking chair, her feet propped on the footstool Carol had reupholstered in the same fabric as the curtains she had made. The transformation to the baby's nursery was nothing short of amazing. A month before, the room had held boxes of unassembled furniture, and Tess had hastily selected some room décor from an online store and put it on her wish list. When Carol had offered her seamstress skills, the animal alphabet items were deleted from the list.

Tess wasn't an I've-got-to-have-it-all type who felt her worth as a mother was related to the number of baby gadgets she owned. Maddie had advised her on the essentials and most of those had been received at the shower. The rest could be ordered and shipped to the house since a trip to the big box baby store was out of the question now.

"I can't believe you got all this done in less than a week." Tess allowed her gaze to wander from the footstool to the matching crib set and finally to the curtains waiting to be hung on the nursery's windows.

Tess could barely thread a needle and didn't own a sewing machine. Her mother had never imparted much domestic knowledge, and when other girls were taking home economics in high school, Tess had enrolled in business classes. Even when Pauline had been in the pits of depression, things somehow got done at home.

Tess had mastered some basic cooking skills and handled the laundry. Several ladies from the neighborhood would often come over while Tess was at school and do light cleaning, though Tess always hated the pitying looks she received from them. Once she started working a part-time job in high school, she used her salary to hire a once-a-week housekeeper. No longer did she have to listen to the neighbors whisper behind her back about pitiful Pauline and her neglected daughter. They knew the truth. They knew Donald Callahan had deserted his family for another woman, but they seemed to have no sympathy for the wife and child left behind.

Tess had lived at home during her undergraduate years, but the law school of her choice was two hundred and fifty miles away. The distance combined with a rigorous classroom and study schedule didn't allow for many trips home. Her hard work, though, had landed her a job back in Atlanta, and she had practiced family law at Hightower, Leggett and Beck ever since.

Pauline had improved during the law school years, and Tess often wondered if she had somehow enabled her mother by doing so much for her. What if she had insisted her mother seek counseling, get out of the house and act like a parent?

Carol's daughters most likely had been prepared for their first period, instead of having to visit the school nurse for help. Carol would probably have spoken up if a group of older girls had ridiculed her daughter's clothes. What if she'd had a mother like Carol Russo? Tess would bet her life savings that Carol had been a room mother, field trip chaperone and Girl Scout leader who baked cookies by the dozen and never forgot a birthday or other special occasion.

All the things Pauline Callahan was not.

Guilt washed over Tess at the unfair comparison. The two women had different circumstances. But not comparing was difficult. It was not difficult, however, to vow that despite having to be a working mother, she would be a different mother to her son than that her mother was to her.

What-ifs were pointless now.

"I have a lot of free time on my hands," Carol said as she smoothed the sheet she'd just put on the crib mattress. "It's just Ben and me, and the house doesn't get very dirty. And I like sewing, so something like this goes quickly."

Carol was so handy at sewing, cooking and all things domestic. And simply put, Tess was not. She had been known to staple a ripped hem back into place. She wondered if Nick compared her to his mother. If so, Tess would surely come up lacking. He had never mentioned anything, but the fact she had never once cooked a meal for him during the two years they had known each other spoke volumes. Or at least it did to her now.

Tess could identify with the time-on-her-hands situation. At least Carol had Ben for company. And even though Nick was gone much of the time, her other children all lived in the metro Atlanta area.

And this led Tess to make more comparisons—the close-knit Russo family as opposed to her single mom who had never fully dealt with her husband's adultery and abandonment. And now, Pauline would not even have the joy of really knowing her grandson.

Carol set a folding stepstool in place by one window and took down the double curtain rod Nick had installed earlier in the week. "I thought maybe you'd be willing to let me share some of my free time with you after the baby arrives." She deftly threaded one rod through the top of the curtain side panels and the other through the valance. She snapped the rods back into place and moved to the second window.

Tess's usual instincts kicked in. "That's very kind, but I don't want to put you out." No matter her baby's grandmother had just made a generous offer that would be most helpful. That independent streak reared its head like a wild stallion resisting a bridle.

"Put me out? Tess, you'd be doing me a favor. I would be able to get out of the house more often and do something more rewarding than sorting books at the library sale or baking for the parish fall festival."

Tess opened her mouth to continue her objection but Carol held up an index finger, shook it from side to side and continued. "I know we've just met, and we met under awkward circumstances. But it is what it is, and you have no clue what you're in for with a newborn baby. I've raised four children and helped with three grandchildren." She patted Tess on the knee. "I know a thing or two about babies."

Carol was absolutely correct. Tess had no clue. She had chosen to work in retail rather than babysit for extra money. It wasn't that she didn't like children. She was merely… Oh hell, why not accept what she had been embarrassed to admit for years: Children scared the living daylights out of her. They were completely helpless at first. Totally dependent. Then they became mobile and nothing in the house below the three-foot mark was safe.

When they learned to talk, it was an endless barrage of meaningless babble before it morphed to "No!" and "Mine!" accompanied by tantrums. The older they got, the more they revolted against authority until they reached puberty and all hell broke loose.

How had Carol survived all that times four and still appeared to be a sane human being? How had her own mother handled it when she had been dealing with her own issues? Guilt sliced through Tess at the memories of how she had sometimes behaved.

But here was Carol, offering to help with dirty diapers, spit-up and who knew what else. Tess had already promised they would be part of the baby's life. And depending on just how much help Carol wanted to offer, this could help her juggle being sandwiched between a child and an aging parent. She would be a fool to turn down Carol's offer. On the other hand, just how awkward would things be without Nick to act as a buffer?

"Give it some thought," Carol said, apparently suspecting Tess's inner turmoil over the idea. "You don't have to decide anything right now. And don't worry. My feelings won't be hurt if you decline. I just thought once Nick left again you might..."

"How have you handled Nick's long absences so well, especially when your other children live so close?" Maybe Carol had some special insight on the subject.

Carol put down the curtain rod she had been ready to hang and sat on the stepstool. A doleful expression crossed her face.

"I won't lie. It's hard. And I feel guilty if I even consider wishing he didn't love his job so much. Isn't that what you're supposed to want for your children? That they lead happy and productive lives? Nick certainly does that." Carol paused, pretended to examine her fingernails, and then sighed deeply. "Maybe I'm to blame. Nicky was born prematurely and I was a smother mother. I coddled him too much. That and the situation with Mellanee probably combined to turn him into a man with a permanently packed suitcase and a passport filled with stamps from every continent."

Mellanee. There was that name again. Tess wanted to know more but was hesitant to ask Nick. Maybe Carol would provide more information. Tess would never know unless she asked. And the worst Carol could do was decline to answer. Or at least Tess hoped that would be the worst response.

Tess drew in a fortifying breath. "That girl, Mellanee. Would you be willing to tell me more about her and what happened? If she's driven Nick's behavior and lifestyle, then maybe I can learn what not to do."

"Honey, I'd tell you more if I knew it. And you've already avoided the biggest mistake." Carol stared directly at Tess's protruding abdomen. "I was so upset over what she did. Upset for myself, upset for Nick. I grieved for that grandchild I'd never hold and finally went to a counselor to seek help. He had me talk about my feelings and write them down when I was at home. Ultimately I had to let it go or I'd have gone mad because there was nothing I could do to change it."

"I wish I could change how I handled this," Tess said, rubbing her right side where the baby's foot lodged under her rib cage. When Carol shot her an alarmed look, Tess quickly clarified. "Don't even think that. He was unplanned, but he's definitely wanted. I went through about a month of denial then just about the time I really accepted I was pregnant, I had to move my mother to an Alzheimer's facility." Tess's voice cracked.

"That must have been difficult. My mother died from a massive stroke about five years ago. She died quickly, thank goodness. She was such an active woman and would not have liked being an invalid. But I can't imagine having a parent with Alzheimer's. It would be like losing them twice—first to the dementia and then later to…" Carol's voice trailed off. The two women sat in silence until Carol broke it.

"Think about my offer." Carol rose and moved to the window. "Now let me finish getting this room ready for my grandson."

*****

"Give me twenty minutes to talk to her," Tess explained as she and Nick walked to her mother's room. "Then come in." Twenty minutes was about the duration of Pauline's concentration, and Tess prayed she'd be able to get it across that she was going to be a grandmother and then introduce Nick.

Tess knew this would be her last visit with her mother before the baby came, and she'd called ahead to ask the nurse about her mother's mental condition that day. Had Pauline been in one of her overly confused and agitated states, Tess would have declined to visit.

But when the nurse said Pauline was having a good day, Tess dressed as quickly as she could and they headed for Waterford Village after eating a quick lunch.

"What if she asks me questions I don't have the answer for?" Nick asked with a hint of panic in his voice.

"To be honest, I think we're going to just have to play it by ear. I'll do as much of the talking as I have to." Tess tried to sound reassuring even though she had the same worries.

"Are you sure you even want to do this? We can go back home now if you think it's going to upset her too much. And I certainly don't want you and the baby put in danger if this gets too emotional."

"No, I really don't want to have this conversation with her, but I feel like I owe it to her to at least try and make her understand what's going on and why I might not be able to visit again for a while."

In her heart, Tess knew her mother hardly remembered her visits anyway. The dementia was becoming increasingly worse, and Tess knew it was only a matter of time before she'd have to transfer her mother to the lock-down wing for her own safety. She had begun wandering away from her room, and just a few days before, she'd become lost on her way to the dining room, a trip she had made three times daily for the past few months.

Tess knew today's visit was a risky move, but her conscience had won out and she'd take her chances.

"It'll be okay. I know it will," she told Nick as much to reassure him as herself.

It has to be okay, Tess prayed fervently.

"I'll do whatever you need me to do," Nick said, squeezing her hand gently in a show of support.

When they reached the door to her mother's room, Nick gave Tess's hand another little squeeze and then checked his watch. "Twenty minutes, right?"

Tess nodded and then rapped softly on the door, which stood ajar.

"Hello, Mama," Tess called out.

Pauline glanced up from her easy chair where she sat looking at a magazine. Her once-dark hair was now snow white and cut into a short, easy-to-manage bob. Her brown eyes frequently contained a look of confusion. Despite her years, she had a smooth, creamy complexion that many women only achieved with the help of a plastic surgeon. Her hands, however, belied her age. The joints were knotted with arthritis and her veins showed blue through the thin skin.

"Tessie. What a surprise. I didn't expect you to come back and visit again today."

Time held no real meaning for Pauline Callahan now. She could remember events from her childhood, but not that Tess's last visit had been a week ago and not earlier that day.

"I have some news for you so I thought I'd come back and tell you." Tess knew she might as well play along because it was pointless to argue. It only upset her mother and that, in turn, upset Tess.

"Oh, I love good news. It is good news, isn't it? I don't like bad news. There's so much bad news on the television today. It reminds me of when the president was assassinated and all we heard for weeks was the reports about that."

"Yes, Mama, it's good news," Tess explained patiently, mentally ticking off the minutes and desperately wanting to tell her mother everything before Nick came into the room. "Remember how I told you I was going to have a baby?"

Pauline cast a glance at Tess's abdomen and a puzzled look crossed her face. "I don't remember that, dear. But I can see that you're in a family way. What did I wear to your wedding? I'm sure I would have worn something in a peach or rose color since that goes so well with my coloring."

"You do look good in those colors, Mama." Tess decided to avoid the wedding question altogether. With her mother's limited memory, anything she told her would soon be forgotten. "The baby is due pretty soon, so I might not be able to visit again for a while. Probably not until after the baby arrives. But I'll bring him to see you just as soon as I can."

"Him? You already know it's a little boy?"

"A little boy, Mama. And I'm going to name him Michael after Grandpa Mike. His middle name is going to be Reece—your maiden name."

Her grandfather had been seventy-five years old when his son-in-law left his wife and daughter for a younger woman. Tess's grandmother had died from cancer before Tess had been born. In spite of his grief, Mike Reece had stepped in and provided as much fatherly support and advice as he could, attending Tess's piano recitals and clapping as loudly as anyone when she had graduated at the top of her high school class. He'd been so proud of her acceptance to college and law school, but sadly he had died in his sleep at the ripe old age of ninety, just three months before Tess graduated from law school.

"My daddy was a good man," Pauline said, taking the conversation in a different direction. "He worked the night shift, and I only saw him in the morning before I'd leave for school. I'd sing a song for him and he would give me a penny to buy candy. Do you know what I sang to him?"

Tess checked her watch again. She didn't have long to explain to her mother about Nick before he came through the door. She knew the song, but also knew that it wouldn't matter if she replied in the affirmative because her mother would answer anyway and sing, just like she'd done dozens of times before. But she had to try and interrupt this once.

"Yes, Mama. You sang 'Life is Just a Bowl of Cherries' and you taught me to sing it too."

"Your father never gave you a penny for singing to him." Pauline's smile disappeared.

And life had not been a bowl of cherries for Pauline Callahan.

"Remember I said I had good news?" Tess asked in an effort to steer the conversation back on track. "I brought my baby's father here to meet you today."

"Oh, wonderful." The smile returned, but only briefly. "It's not that dreadful Carson boy, is it? He seemed like such a hooligan, and I wasn't at all thrilled when he asked you to the senior prom. You wore a peach dress to that, didn't you?" Pauline paused and shook her head as if to jiggle the memories back into place. "I just don't remember if I wore that color to your wedding."

That hooligan had been the mayor's son. Steve Carson now had a couple of doctorates and was CEO of a high-tech company in Silicon Valley where he lived with his wife and three children in a home that had been featured in a major architecture magazine the year before. He wasn't Tess's type, but he had been the only boy to ask her to the prom, so she had said yes.

"You should be glad you didn't marry him. I'll bet he's in prison now." Pauline continued, and Tess began to question whether she should just step outside and tell Nick to stay in the hall. Her mother's thought patterns had deteriorated so much that holding a normal conversation was like picking your way through a corn maze, never knowing at each turn if that route would take you out or to a dead end.

"I think you'll like him, Mama." Once again Tess tried to direct the conversation back to the subject at hand. "He's going to make a great father." An absent one, but a good one nonetheless.

"I remember how excited I was when I found out I was going to have you. You were quite a surprise, Tessie. Your father and I had tried for years and years to have a baby, and I'd given up hope. Then you came along. I wanted your father to come into the delivery room with me. They were starting to do that then you know. I wanted to take those classes and have him with me to see this miracle, but he said he wasn't sure he would be able to be there since his job kept him so busy."

Given that her father had abandoned them for another woman, Tess would have been willing to bet good money her father would have felt inconvenienced at having to be of assistance to his laboring wife and chose instead to leave her to her own devices.

"Is your husband going to be with you?"

Before Tess could answer, Nick walked into the room and stood just inside the doorway. He shoved his hands into his pockets, and a look of both uncertainty and fear filled his face.

Pauline looked at him, puzzled by the visitor to her room. Then a broad smile filled her face. "Donald. Here you are. Just in time to hear all about Tess's baby. We're going to be grandparents, Donald. Isn't that wonderful?"

Of all the scenarios Tess had imagined, this particular one had never crossed her mind. And from the look of trepidation on Nick's face, he had no idea how to proceed.

"It's going to be a little boy too, and she's naming him after my father. That's okay, isn't it? Because she can name the next one after you. I think there's still a trunk of Tess's toys in the attic and you can hang a swing from the big maple tree in the backyard. Don't just stand there, Donald. Give your daughter a hug."

*****

Nick moved to Tess's side and pulled her into a side-to-side embrace. He had expected an awkward situation, trying to explain about being the father of Tess's baby. But he never imagined he would be mistaken for someone else—Tess's father if he had guessed correctly from the context of her mother's comments.

Tess had only spoken about her father once, and not in flattering terms. The white-haired woman who'd just mistaken him for someone else was a dozen or so years older than his own mother. What a difference that must have made in Tess's life. And what a difference it made now. She had a mother with dementia and a long-gone father, which was such a contrast to his family. His parents were as much in love as the day they had married— no, more.

Now he was experiencing more than a moment of regret for giving his mother such grief when she nagged him about settling down and giving her more grandchildren.

Tess's mother would most likely forget she even had a grandchild, the memory of it stolen by dementia. His mother, however, would know his child. If she treated this baby like she did her other grandchildren, the child would know an abundance of love and laughter. And Nick had no doubts that would be the case.

His regret was also compounded by guilt because this new job opportunity—if it was offered and if he accepted—meant he would have to leave Tess, perhaps before the baby even arrived. Would she lump him in the same category as her father? Or would he at least be a notch above because he did care about his child and would provide for him even if he was working in Timbuktu?

"I think it's wonderful the baby will be named after your father," Nick adlibbed. "He was a good man, and I know he would be honored to have his great-grandchild named after him."

"I just don't understand where your husband is, Tess." Pauline shifted in her chair, glancing toward the door. "Didn't you say he was coming to visit me? A woman in your condition shouldn't be traipsing about alone. I'm disappointed in him. What did you say his name was again?"

Nick could feel Tess tense in his arms. He could not imagine how she must feel at this moment. If it was his mother, he'd be devastated. Of course there was always the possibility that one day one or both of his parents would be in this very situation.

"Don't be disappointed in him, Mama," Tess reassured her. "He's at home fixing up the baby's room and getting everything ready."

Pauline stood and pointed her finger at Tess. "I have something I want to give you for the baby. Wait here and I'll get it." She disappeared into the adjoining bedroom.

"I'm so sorry about this, Nick," Tess apologized after her mother left the room. "I never imagined she would think you were my father. Thank you for playing along."

"And she probably won't remember this tomorrow, right?"

Tess nodded and leaned against him, exhaustion evident in her expression and the slump of her shoulders. He needed to get her home soon.

"Here it is," Pauline exclaimed as she returned to her sitting room. "It's a little music box I'd like for your baby to have."

She held out a heart-shaped box made of Italian inlaid wood. She opened the lid and let it play a few bars of something Nick recognized as a popular movie theme from the sixties.

"Thank you, Mama. I'm sure the baby will love it."

"You look tired, dear," her mother commented. "Donald, I think you need to take her home and let her rest. She's in a delicate condition you know. And when you get back, I'll fix us a nice dinner."

Nick could see that Tess *was* tired, both physically and emotionally. Her mother's rapidly deteriorating condition along with her own problem pregnancy had taken a tremendous toll. And he had to make sure neither Tess nor the baby paid the price.

"Yes, I'm tired, so I'll go on home now. But I need to use your bathroom first."

When Tess returned much too quickly to have actually used the bathroom, he sent her an inquisitive look.

"I'll explain," she mouthed, and then she hugged her mother and left the room quickly with Nick on her heels.

Tess was strangely quiet until they were almost home.

"I had to put the music box back in her room. Walter gave it to her for her birthday one year. 'Moon River' is her favorite song. I knew she'd forget she gave the box to me, and then she'd accuse one of the staff of stealing it. I don't want her forgetfulness to cause any trouble. I'll just have to remember to tell Walter about it in case she mentions something about it. He'll understand."

Nick nodded in agreement, sad that Tess had been forced to deal with yet another complication of her mother's failing memory.

As soon as they reached home, Tess maneuvered up the stairs to her room, toed off her shoes and crawled onto the bed. Nick had learned to read her moods well enough to know at this point he should leave her alone except to bring her a dinner tray. After feeding Alley and changing her water, he fixed a simple meal of soup and a sandwich, and when he returned later to collect the tray, Tess had barely touched the food.

"Can you stand guard outside the bathroom while I shower?" she asked. "Then I just want to go to sleep."

Nick complied with her request though he still wasn't able to sit outside the bathroom door without wondering what she looked like naked and her belly swollen with his child. He might never know, but it didn't stop him from speculating.

After settling her into bed, where she fell asleep almost before he had turned the off the light, Nick retreated to the den to do a little soul searching.

He could ask himself a thousand questions and play the *woulda, shoulda, coulda* game forever, but none of that could change the facts.

He pulled his cell phone from his pocket and dialed Bella. Maybe talking to her about the possible job offer might help shed some light on things.

After some chit chat and a report on Tess's condition, Nick changed the subject.

"Pete Clark called about an assignment."

"Already? I thought you had some vacation time coming."

"I do," he said. "But this is a big story and Pete said he wants only the best crew covering it. I should feel flattered, and I do, but I don't. I know that sounds crazy."

"Doesn't sound crazy at all," she replied. "But that's going to go over with Mom and Tess like a lead balloon," she said, stating the obvious. "What *do* you feel?"

Nick stared blankly at the carpet beneath his feet, silent as he tried to make sense of the emotions coursing through him.

"Are you still there, Nicky?"

"Disappointed. That's what I feel. Disappointed I won't have the balls to turn down the job if it's offered. Disappointed I'll miss my son's birth if I take the job. Disappointed I'll let Tess down when I've kept telling her I'd be there for her."

"Have you told Tess about the offer?"

"No. It's not definite yet, so why get everyone upset over something that might not happen?"

"You mean why should you do today what you can put off until tomorrow? Don't you think Tess has a right to know you might have to walk away at a moment's notice? Are you supposed to be her Lamaze coach?" Bella grilled him like a hard-hitting police interrogator, and he felt like a criminal for what he might have to do.

"Her friend Maddie went to class with her and is supposed to be her coach. But I've read all the books and watched the video, and she said she wanted me there for the birth. So, I guess… I mean…I don't know. I don't know if I'll be there as a participant or just a spectator." Frustration over all the unknown factors in his life gnawed at him.

The thought of watching a child being born—his child being born—both captivated and terrified him.

"You need to tell her. Warn her so she can make plans in case she's counting on you to be there at the birth and to be around to help once the baby is born. It's the decent thing to do, Nick. And maybe…" Bella paused for a few moments before resuming the conversation. "Maybe you should talk to your boss about your situation and explain that you might need some extra time to deal with family matters."

"What? Bella, if I'm offered this job and then turn it down, I'd be committing career suicide." Nick stood and paced the length of the den. In his profession, staying in the public eye was critical for success. He'd seen several great photographers' careers dwindle to nothing because illness or injury had taken them out of commission just long enough for the powers that be to forget about them when the time came to staff the next big assignment. He hadn't worked his ass off to give it all up now.

But Bella had a point. He couldn't leave Tess in a bind. She had to be prepared to care for the baby properly, and that included help both in the hospital and after she and the baby came home. He felt trapped between that proverbial rock and hard place.

"I'm not telling you to turn down the assignment, which if I understand correctly, you don't even have yet. I'm just suggesting you explore your options, and for heaven's sake please give Tess a heads-up that she might need to make other plans."

"I will," Nick conceded. "I'll talk to her soon."

"Tonight, Nick. Talk to her tonight."

"She's already asleep. The trip to visit her mother wore her out, and based on how quickly she fell asleep, I don't think she's going to budge until tomorrow morning."

"Then tell her tomorrow. As soon as possible," Bella said with big-sister firmness. "I'm speaking as a woman, and we like to know what's going on. We like order and some sense of security. You might be able to throw two pairs of underwear and some socks into a backpack at the last minute and fly halfway around the world, but a mother and a newborn need a heck of a lot more than that."

Nick knew his sister was right and grumbled something to that effect before hanging up and heading to the kitchen to grab a beer.

He flopped onto the sofa and punched the remote, bringing the TV to life. He flipped to his favorite channels but couldn't concentrate on any of the programming. In his mind, he kept replaying the visit with Tess's mother and his conversation with Bella. Tess had more on her plate than anyone deserved. And he shouldn't be the one to add another serving to the load.

*****

The sound of Tess's crying woke Nick, and a quick glance at the alarm clock next to his bed showed it was half past eleven. He imagined the tears stemmed from the upsetting visit with her mother, but in the back of his mind he was remembering his sister's advice to tell Tess about the possible job offer.

If she was this upset now, how much more upset might she get if he told her he could be called away at any moment? He allowed his conscience to be convinced that the best course of action was to wait until he knew something for sure. If the job didn't pan out, then there was nothing to tell. If it did, he'd make sure she had all the help she needed. He knew for sure his mother had offered to help, and just as surely, she'd be mad as hell at him for his actions.

But why was everyone mad at him? Why wasn't anyone mad at Tess for not letting them know about the baby sooner? He'd been kept in the dark and then constantly blamed for everything.

Nick had been thrust right into the middle of the situation purely by chance. He could have walked away with a "nice to see you again" and left Tess to her own devices. Instead he had done his damnedest to make sure Tess was cared for and was prepared for the baby's arrival. Hell yeah, it sucked that he had forfeited an airline ticket to St. Kitts and the deposit on a beachside villa in order to stay in Atlanta when Wendy didn't work out. He had never mentioned it to anyone, especially Tess. She felt guilty enough about not taking better care of herself prior to the store incident. No use giving her more to possibly feel guilty about.

He rolled over and pulled the pillow over his head to drown out the sound of Tess's sobs, but when the pillow failed to do the job, he became more concerned. He slipped from the bed and padded in his bare feet to her bedroom door.

"It's me," he said, knocking softly on the partially open door. Then he felt incredibly stupid, because who else would it have been? Burglars didn't announce themselves. "Can I get you anything? A glass of water? Extra pillows?"

A cure for Alzheimer's and a baby daddy who isn't an adrenaline junkie and drops everything on a moment's notice to take photos in the most godforsaken places around the globe?

Tess sniffled and in the moonlight shining through the window, he could see her reach for a tissue.

"I'm okay. It's just the hormones again I guess."

Nick moved closer to the bed, drawn by her vulnerability and the attraction he could not avoid. "Those damned hormones." He dragged the words out. "They get blamed for an awful lot, don't they?"

Tess seemed to want to share. "It's a lot easier to blame hormones than to blame some of the choices I've made," she confessed. "And I sure can't blame my mother because she didn't ask to have Alzheimer's." She dabbed at her eyes and crumpled the tissue in her hand.

"If it makes you feel better," Nick said, "you're not alone in the blame game. We've probably all made bad choices in our lives." The mattress dipped when he sat on the corner of the bed.

"I used to blame myself for my parents' divorce. My mother and father were both forty years old when I was born. My arrival completely disrupted their lives. My mother gave up her career as a nurse to stay home with me and she became completely dependent on my father for everything." Tess swiped at her eyes again with the tissue.

"When I was ten years old my father came in one day and announced he was leaving. I watched him pack a couple suitcases, put some stuff from his desk in a box and he drove away. I was too young to understand anything about the divorce. It wasn't until I was much older that I found out he left for a woman twenty years younger than him. I guess he was going through some sort of midlife crisis and this blonde bimbo thought she was getting the catch of the century. Funny thing is, a man who will cheat on his wife will cheat on his mistress too. And I've heard my father has left a trail of broken hearts in his wake." She sighed heavily.

Nick pushed off the bed and walked around to the other side. He reached for the bedside lamp.

"Don't." Her voice sounded almost desperate. "It's so much easier to spill your guts in the dark. That way you don't have to see the pity in other people's faces."

Nick slipped into the bed beside her and helped her get into a more comfortable position. He propped against the headboard, brushed a lock of her hair away from her tear-stained face and tucked it behind her ear. "That's an awful lot for a ten-year-old to carry around," he said softly.

"So there was my mother at age fifty with a young daughter and uncertain job prospects. She really struggled financially. After I got out of law school, I looked at her divorce settlement. My mother must have had the worst attorney in the state of Georgia. She should have been awarded half their property and assets plus part of my father's retirement, and she got virtually nothing, including no alimony. I would never let a client sign a settlement like that, especially where such blatant adultery and abandonment was involved. And his child support payments were a joke. The state mandated how much he had to pay, but when he didn't, my mother didn't have the funds to file contempt charges against him."

Silence loomed like a dark spell between them until Nick broke it. "I never knew any of that about you and your mother."

"You never asked."

"I guess I was always too busy having fun to think about anything else," he admitted.

"I'm not sure I'd have told you if you had asked. I've always kept my private life just that—private. I didn't want people feeling sorry for me. I wanted to succeed like hell and prove to myself that I could make it on my own and not need anyone else. Maybe…" Tess paused.

"You *have* succeeded, Tess. You're one of the strongest women I know."

"Maybe I succeeded a little too well and got carried away. Maybe that's what put me in this situation." Tess huffed out a wry laugh. "It's ironic, isn't it? Because I wanted so badly *not* to have to depend on anyone, I've ended up having to depend on everybody."

Nick took her hand in his and gave it a gentle squeeze. "I'm sorry you had to go through that. It's made me realize how incredibly lucky I am to be part of such a wonderful family, and I want you to know that they all consider you part of the family now too."

"I really enjoyed the visits with your mother. She and your dad have been so sweet to do so much for me. I mean, the nursery is beautiful, like something out of a magazine."

"My mom loves to do stuff like that. She's done all she can do at their house and dad threatened to sell her sewing machine on Craigslist if she even mentions another project to him. She really should have been a professional decorator."

"She has a great eye for things. I'd have never thought about the color combinations she came up for the nursery, and I love it." Tess heaved a sigh. "I just wish my mother could understand what's going on. She used to hint about maybe one day being a grandmother. And I think I cheated her out of knowing me because I became so focused on not ending up like her. I had a deep need to ensure that I had a career and money and everything required to take care of myself and not have to depend on anyone, man or woman, to help me."

"That's not necessarily a bad goal for any woman to have. It's an uncertain world out there."

"Yeah," she said, "but maybe I was a bit too independent. Pride can be a destructive thing if you let it get in the way of what's right. I really did want to tell you about the baby, but after I tried and tried to call and you didn't call back, I figured you had moved on to another woman and I was yesterday's news. I certainly didn't want to leave a message saying, 'Hi, Daddy. Guess what? I'm pregnant so please call me back,' because that's just a little abrupt. I thought you deserved to be told in person."

The bed shook a little as Nick laughed. "Well, I sure found out in person, didn't I? I wish you could have seen the look on your face when you turned around and saw me standing there."

"You looked pretty shocked yourself. I don't know why I wore that particular shirt that day because it fits snugly and you can't miss that I'm pregnant. If I'd worn…well, it doesn't really matter, does it? My mother has seen me all though the pregnancy and she's never once asked me directly if I was going to have a baby. Then today she thought you were my father. I'm so sorry, Nick. If I'd had any idea she would think you were someone else, I'd have never asked you to come into her room."

"It's okay. I understand." He continued to stroke her hair.

"I just wonder sometimes why she never said yes to Walter's proposals. He's the kindest, most unselfish man, and he clearly loves her."

Nick said nothing. Perhaps her mother had refused Walter because she had already been emotionally devastated once. Trust was a hard commodity to come by when yours had been so ruthlessly betrayed.

Nick knew that firsthand.

*****

Tess yawned loudly. She was tired but wasn't sure she would be able to fall back to sleep. So many notions whirled through her mind. Often she joked about her chattering monkey brain and how much trouble she had shutting it down every night. Her thoughts were usually about her clients and upcoming trials. Now the monkey had new worries to chatter about when she closed her eyes and tried to sleep.

"Would you stay with me? Let me prop against you like before?" she asked when Nick began to move off the bed. "I promise I won't complain about, you know." She waved her hand in the direction of his lower body. "That morning thing."

Nick chuckled. "Sure, and I'll try not to let *that morning thing* get in your way." He slipped under the covers and stretched out behind Tess.

She took a deep breath and contemplated her next statement. It could have consequences. Oh hell, who was she trying to fool? It *would* have consequences. Consequences she wasn't entirely sure would be so bad. "And if you wanted to wrap your arm around me, I wouldn't complain about that either."

Minutes passed that seemed like hours, and Tess worried she had pushed too far. She had asked so much already, and he had given more than she had asked. He would be leaving for his next assignment soon, most likely before the baby arrived, and she wanted to savor the time they had together. Who knew when he would be back? And just how involved would he be in their lives when he returned?

Uncharacteristically, she thought, why worry about what might be? She'd concentrate on the present.

She sensed the heat from his skin before she felt his touch. Nick reached out and let his hand rest gently on her hip. She covered it with her own and moved both to a spot on her abdomen where the baby moved.

Before long he'd be moving outside of her, living in the room painted by his grandfather and decorated by his grandmother. And he would be sleeping in the crib assembled by his father. But would his father be there to watch him sleep?

Chapter Twelve

No matter how many times he felt the baby move inside Tess, Nick still marveled at the miracle of it. Soon that little miracle would join the world. He would be able to look into his son's eyes and get to know him—unless he got the job halfway around the world and had to depart as suddenly as he had the night they'd conceived the baby.

One reality colliding with another didn't sit well and weighed heavily on him. The conversation with Bella still resonated in his thoughts, and his conscience nagged him to sit down with Tess and let her know what might happen.

He'd halfway told Bella he would talk to Tess in the morning, and he dreaded the confrontation, which was exactly what it would turn into. He would argue that he had to make a living so he could help support his child. He couldn't help that making that living took him all over the world. And Tess would argue right back that... Just what would her argument be? That she expected nothing from him and was getting exactly nothing? That he was deserting her like her father had?

He wasn't deserting anyone. He wasn't leaving her for another woman. He would provide financial support and be as present in his child's life as his job would allow. When the baby was old enough, they could Skype so Michael would know what his father looked like. And Tess would argue... He could play this mental version of a courtroom cross-examination forever, but it would not solve anything.

The baby shifted again and so did Tess. She arched her spine slightly then reached around with her hand to rub at her lower back before becoming still again. She repeated the arch, back rub and shift several times before Nick realized it was a pattern.

"Here, let me," he said, pressing his thumb into the small of her back and massaging firmly. When she groaned, he let up on the pressure. "Sorry. I didn't mean to hurt you."

"No, don't stop. It feels good. That was a good groan."

"Thank you for clarifying that, because I haven't learned to differentiate between a good groan and a bad one." He resumed the massage, balling up his fist and running the heel of his palm along her spine.

"A good one is usually accompanied by a smile," she explained.

"It's dark," he said. "And you're facing away from me."

"Then I'll try to remember in the future to tell you if it's good or bad. How's that?"

"I think that'll work." He stopped and flexed his fingers a few times. "Need more?"

"Mmm-hmmm," she answered. "I guess it's just part of being pregnant. It's all been on–the-job training. I've read all the books, but everything in them is just an estimate since every pregnancy is different. Some women have morning sickness and some don't. Some gain lots of weight and some gain very little. Your feet might swell or not. You might have back aches at night or you might sleep just fine."

"Have you had this every night? Why didn't you tell me? I'd have massaged your back for you."

"Only once in a while. Usually the baby shifts position and it stops. Tonight it's worse, but he's getting bigger and doesn't have much room to move around."

Anxiety rippled through Nick, and he willed his voice to remain calm. "Everything is okay, though, isn't it? I mean, I don't need to call the doctor, do I?"

"I'm not having contractions, if that's what you're asking. I seem to always have something out of whack lately, and tonight it's my back. And my emotions." Tess's voice weighed heavy with exhaustion.

Nick leaned toward her and pressed a kiss lightly to the side of her neck before resuming the back massage. "I think you're entitled to both. You've been through a lot."

An unexpected and problematic pregnancy. Her mother's worsening dementia. How many burdens did the universe expect this woman to shoulder?

An hour after he entered her room, Tess finally drifted back to sleep. He listened to her soft breathing, remembering her earlier statement about having to depend on everyone. A sensation of satisfaction filled him from knowing she had been able to depend on him tonight and also the day before during the visit to see her mother.

Nick wasn't used to being depended upon and generally shied away from anything not related to his work or immediate family. And even then, his family often came in second place to the job.

Maybe he should call Pete and tell him to take his name out of the hat for Bulgaria. Surely one assignment couldn't make that much difference in his career. And there would be another big story somewhere he could take on to make up for this one. Wouldn't there?

Or perhaps he should consider resigning from *Earth Events* altogether and look for something that would keep him located closer to Atlanta—or at least within the United States. That way he'd never be more than a day's flight away from Tess and the baby.

Exhaustion was not conducive to the decision-making process. He still had plenty of time—four more weeks until Tess's due date, and he hoped he had at least that long before he had to decide about the assignment—*if* he was selected.

Nick closed his eyes and let the weariness take over. Tomorrow he would talk with Tess and tell her about his conversation with Pete. But now he would sleep.

*****

A strange sensation woke Tess. A quick glance at the clock revealed the time: one o'clock. At first she wasn't sure if it was something real or part of the dream she'd been having about Nick. She lay still for a moment, then wiggled her fingers and toes and realized what had caused her to wake. A long groan escaped from her throat.

Nick shifted and mumbled. "Was that a good groan again?"

"I…I'm not sure," she said hesitantly.

"What do you mean you're not sure? It's your groan. You should know. Are you smiling?"

"Okay, then. I think it's a bad groan because I think my water just broke."

"Do you just think or do you know for sure?" Nick had scrambled to a sitting position and rubbed his eyes.

Tess touched the front of her nightgown and found it was soaking wet. But perhaps the baby had just punched her bladder and caused her to lose control. He had sat on it almost from the day of conception.

"Help me to the bathroom and maybe I can tell," she instructed, explaining her bladder theory. Thank goodness she'd had the presence of mind to put a plastic cover on her mattress right after the doctor had put her on bed rest.

From the bathroom she could hear Nick stripping the linens from the bed. When she couldn't control the liquid seeping from her, she accepted what she'd suspected all along.

"Are you okay?" Nick called from outside the bathroom door.

"Will you please call Dr. Merrell and tell him I'm pretty sure my water has broken?" Tess tried to keep her voice steady, but a quiver of fear crept through. "And will you bring me a clean nightgown and panties and my heavy robe?"

"I've put them beside the sink," he said moments later. "And I'm calling the doctor now. Do you need me to help you? No? Oh, yes. Dr. Merrell. This is Nick Russo calling for Tess Callahan. Her water broke while she was asleep."

Tess could hear Nick pacing in the bedroom as she donned the dry clothes, stuffing several sanitary napkins into her panties to absorb the trickle of amniotic fluid.

"No, no contractions that she's mentioned. No blood on the sheets. Mmmm-hmmm. Okay. Yeah, sure. We can do that," she heard him say. "We'll see you at the hospital."

She returned to the bedroom and found Nick putting on jeans and a sweatshirt. He pulled on a pair of white socks and jammed his feet into his running shoes.

"Come on," he said, taking her by the elbow. "Dr. Merrell is going to meet us at the ER and figure out what's going on."

"I need shoes."

She saw his gaze sweep to her bare feet, and she wiggled her toes in the carpet.

"Do you want socks and shoes or—"

"My slippers will be fine. It's not like I'm walking to the hospital. They probably got pushed under the bed when I got up."

Nick swept his hand back and forth under the bed until he found both slippers, and then let her hold onto him while she slid her feet into them. At the top of the stairs, Nick paused.

"Wait. Where's your suitcase?"

Pack Suitcase was the top item on the to-do list for the following week. "I haven't packed it yet. I was going to do it this week. It's on the top shelf of my closet. Get it for me and I can pack something quickly."

"No. We need to get to the hospital now. You can make me a list after we get there, and I'll bring it to you."

"It'll only take a few minutes," Tess argued, turning toward her room. "I know exactly what I need to pack."

Nick stepped in front of her and put both hands on her shoulders. "Minutes count, sweetheart. And you don't have any to spare right now. Let's go, and I'll get the suitcase later."

Tess heard an urgency in his voice that almost frightened her— not that she wasn't frightened already. But she had to believe Nick only had her best interest at heart as well as the welfare of their baby. It wasn't as if she needed the new gowns and robe she had received as shower gifts right away.

He guided her downstairs and into the car after grabbing his jacket from the back of a kitchen chair and retrieving her purse from the kitchen table where she'd left it that afternoon.

They rode for the first few miles in silence. She knew she was far enough along for the baby to be well developed, but she had hoped to carry him to full term. "I shouldn't have gone to visit my mother today. If I wasn't so stubborn and had followed the doctor's orders, this wouldn't be happening."

Nick reached over, grabbed her hand and brought it to his lips for a soft kiss. "I don't think that's what caused your water to break, if that's actually what has happened. I think maybe Junior is just anxious to come out and meet his beautiful mother."

"You're just saying that to be nice. I know you'd rather tell me 'I told you so.' Go ahead and say it."

He kissed her hand again, his lips lingering against her skin a little longer this time. "This isn't your fault, Tess. So stop blaming yourself. If you *are* going into labor, you need to focus all your energy on having this baby."

Middle-of-the-night traffic was light, and they arrived at the hospital without incident. Nick pulled into the ER entrance and they were met by two nurses who whisked Tess inside while he parked the car.

The admitting staff bombarded Tess with questions as they helped her into a wheelchair and took her to an examination room. She had pre-registered with the hospital so it took only moments to retrieve her files on the computer.

"Ms. Callahan, my name is Paula. Dr. Merrell is on his way, but in the meantime I can check you to see if your water has indeed broken." Paula and another nurse helped her onto an exam table and draped her with a sheet. "Let's take a look here," she said.

Tess couldn't see anything from the uncomfortable position flat on her back, but she could feel the nurse's gloved hand against her bare skin.

"And I'm Debbie," the other nurse explained as she swiped a digital thermometer across Tess's forehead and noted the result on the computer. Next she wrapped a blood pressure cuff around Tess's arm and soon the cuff began to tighten.

"I bet it'll set a new world record," Tess remarked, trying to laugh but failing to achieve the humorous tone she'd hoped for.

"No," Debbie replied. "It's pretty normal, all things considered. Take deep breaths and try to relax. I know that sounds impossible, but you need to let us take care of everything now."

Just then a woman stuck her head into the exam room. "There's a Nick Russo out here asking for you, Ms. Callahan. He isn't listed on any of your paperwork so I can't let him back here without your okay."

Apprehension knotted tightly inside her and Nick was the surefire antidote to that. "Please let him come in. He's the…he's my… I need him with me."

Need him. Words she never thought she would utter. How had she thought she could do this alone? Tess had prided herself on the ability to manage her life, and pregnancy had challenged her management skills to the limit, especially after she had been put on bed rest.

In a few days she would be home with a newborn, juggling feeding schedules and diaper changes. And several months after that, she would add her job into the equation. Her work day wasn't always a nice, neat eight-to-five schedule. A mediation could run long. An appeal could need a last-minute extension. Even with her top-notch paralegal, she couldn't always count on leaving the office at five o'clock.

She still had to find a nanny. How flexible would she be? Insecurity and fear, emotions she'd conquered long ago, swept over her and the tears gathering behind her lids spilled down her cheeks.

And what if the baby had an extended hospital stay due to his early arrival? She hadn't even taken that possibility into consideration.

Moments later Nick was ushered into the exam room and took a seat at Tess's side. He brushed her hair away from her forehead and wiped away the tears with the pad of his thumb.

"Has the doctor been here yet?" he asked.

"He's on the way," Tess answered, trying to keep her voice steady but not succeeding.

"Your water *has* broken so we're taking you up to the Labor and Delivery wing," Paula said. "We'll let Dr. Merrell know to come straight there."

"So. This is it, huh?" Nick asked nervously.

Tess nodded and her independent streak reared its head. "But you don't have to be in the labor and delivery room with me if you don't want to. I can call Maddie and—"

Nick grasped her hand and barely squeezed it. "There isn't any place I'd rather be right now. Let Maddie sleep. I'll call her in the morning, but I do need to call my mother now."

Tess sent him a quizzical look. "At this ungodly hour?"

"She made me promise, and you know my mother." A sheepish grin lifted the corners of his mouth. "She and Pop will probably rush right over here even though there's nothing to do but pace the waiting room floor."

The clock read three in the morning by the time they reached the Labor and Delivery suite. Dr. Merrell had arrived at the hospital and greeted them in the room. He studied Tess's records while a nurse helped her put on a standard-issue gown that snapped across the shoulders and tied up the back. Tess settled into the hospital bed with pillows added and adjusted to achieve as much comfort as possible. One nurse inserted an IV into the back of her hand and another hooked her to a fetal monitor.

"No, Mom. You don't have to be here. It's the middle of the night and I only called because I knew you'd disown me if I didn't," he argued into the phone. "Yes, she's fine, or as fine as a woman having a baby can be."

He glanced toward Tess, shrugged and rolled his eyes dramatically. "I'll tell her. Love you too." He shoved the phone in his back pocket and returned to Tess's side.

"Is all this normal?" Nick asked, gesturing to the array of machinery behind the bed. "Or is there a problem because the baby is early?"

The doctor patted Nick on the shoulder. "Stop worrying, Daddy. Everything looks good right now. He's going to be a bit on the small side, but his vitals are fine. See here?" He pointed to one of the monitors. "That's his heartbeat and it's right where it should be. And here's where the uterine contractions will be displayed once Tess goes into active labor. You'll be able to watch the progress of a contraction and help Tess breathe through it. You're still planning a natural birth, aren't you?"

At Nick's wide-eyed look, Tess answered that she was.

"But what if I screw up?" Nick asked. "I mean, I read the book, but…"

"You'll do just fine," one of the nurses attending to Tess assured him. "My name is Karen and I'll be here through the labor and delivery. You just follow her lead and pay close attention to the monitors and everything will work out."

"And I'm going to the doctor's lounge to nap until we get to show time." At Nick's worried look, the doctor issued more assurances. "I'll just be down the hall and Karen will text me if necessary. She's one of the best nurses in this hospital. Tess and the baby are in good hands."

An hour later the first contraction grabbed Tess and a quick glance at the monitor showed a slight blip on the screen. She inhaled deeply through her nose and let the breath out through her mouth in a long hiss.

"I think it's starting," she said when the contraction ended. "It was just a little cramping, but I guess that's how it begins." She had read all the books and attended classes. And until this moment she had felt completely prepared for childbirth. One small contraction, however, shredded her confidence and sent her emotions into overdrive. And it galled her to react that way—especially in front of Nick.

She tamped down the anxiety, put on her best courtroom face and took a long, deep breath for relaxation.

An hour later, much stronger contractions held her in their grip. "I think we need to change breathing," she announced, squeezing

Nick's hand. From that point on, every subsequent contraction became a little stronger and the time between contractions shortened.

Nick held her hand, wiped her face with a damp cloth and watched the monitor to talk her through each contraction as she inhaled and exhaled in a slow but rhythmic pattern.

"I'm going to throw up," Tess called out without warning. Karen held a basin under Tess's chin and she vomited into it.

"What's wrong?" Panic showed in Nick's face. "What's happening?"

"Nothing's wrong," Karen assured him as she offered Tess a glass of water to rinse out her mouth. "It's just nature's way of making sure her stomach doesn't have to work at the same time her uterus does."

"You must have skipped that chapter in the book," Tess commented sarcastically. She was grateful Karen had confirmed what she remembered from her reading and that this wasn't some abnormality unique to premature labor. She had enough worry plaguing her without adding to it. "I—"

The beginning of another strong contraction cut off her remark, and this time she squeezed Nick's fingers until he visibly winced.

He watched the monitor and let her know when the contraction had peaked.

"It's almost over. Just a few seconds more. Now take a good deep cleansing breath. Inhale through your nose—"

"I know how to take a damn breath," she snapped as soon as the contraction eased.

"I'm sorry. I'm just trying to help. We should have gone to childbirth classes."

"*I* did," she deadpanned after deliberately exhaling into Nick's face. "With Maddie. You weren't here, remember?"

"Like you'd let me forget," he mumbled.

"Call Maddie about six-thirty? That's when the girls get her up anyway, and she'll be livid if I don't let her know I'm in here."

Nick promised he would just as another contraction began. He talked Tess through it using the line on the monitor.

When the nurse checked her progress at six o'clock, it was apparent Tess's labor was progressing rapidly. "I think we'll have a baby by seven o'clock," Karen predicted. "Eight at the very latest. You're dilating pretty quickly for a first pregnancy, and I think you're going to start transition soon. So be ready. You'll want to push but you can't yet. Just remember your breathing."

Tess felt as if she was caught in a whirlwind. Everything was happening far faster than she had expected. One advantage was she had no time to obsess. She had to remain focused.

"Go ahead and call Maddie now," she instructed Nick. "You won't have time once I start into transition."

*****

Nick tried his damnedest to remember what transition was because it was apparently something important. He pulled his cell phone from his pocket and stepped just outside the labor suite to make the call.

When Jack's groggy voice answered, he explained the situation and asked to speak to Maddie.

"Tess is in labor," he explained when he heard Maddie's sleepy voice on the other end of the line. "I can't talk long because they said she's going into something called transition and I need to get back in there. But Tess wanted you to know. Tell Jack I'm sorry I woke him."

"Thanks for calling, and don't worry about Jack. And Nick," she added, "transition is the last part of labor and it's intense. If you thought the mood swings were bad before, watch out and consider yourself warned. But it's also pretty fast. Jack swears up and down I questioned his parentage when I was in transition and I don't remember saying a word of it. It's hard work to give birth. That's why they call it labor. Just be there for her. And tell her I love her and I'll be there as soon as I can get someone to watch the girls."

"I'll tell her, and thanks for the refresher on transition."

Nick heard Jack's voice in the background along with a muffled conversation.

"Oh, wait. Jack says he'll stay home from work and watch the girls so I should be there in a little bit."

"Thanks, Maddie. Tess will appreciate you being here. You've been a great friend to her."

Much better than I've been.

Nick ended the call and returned to the labor room to face an entirely different woman than the one he had left minutes before.

Pain contorted Tess's face, and she spit out a string of curses like machine gun fire. Under different circumstances he might have commented on the unique way she strung the words together.

"Find a focal point in the room and concentrate on it while you do your transition breathing," Karen directed. "Remember how to do it? It's like this." The nurse began a breathing pattern that sounded like she was puffing out the words *hee hee hee who*.

Pointing at Nick, the nurse delivered an order. "Come over here, please. You're going to have to help her so she doesn't push. Just keep her breathing like I showed her and find something for her to focus her attention on."

As the contraction subsided and Tess slumped back against the pillow, Nick moved the stool so he could face her. Sweat beaded on her forehead and weariness creased her brow. He glanced around for something bright use as a focal point and then caught sight of his reflection in the fetal monitor screen.

He'd pulled on a Great Pumpkin Festival sweatshirt before leaving the house and a bright orange jack-o-lantern dominated the front of it.

"Use this," he said, pointing to his garment. "Look at the pumpkin."

Just then another contraction began, and together they huffed their way through it. "You know where I'd like to shove that pumpkin, don't you?" she asked with a feral grin.

Nick remembered what Maddie had said and took a deep breath. "Close your eyes and rest before the next contraction starts," he suggested, reaching to wipe her forehead again.

She swatted his hand away. "I feel like I'm trying to give birth to a giant pumpkin. Imagine trying to push a jack-o'-lantern through a drinking straw." She reached out and grabbed the waistband of his jeans. "Or maybe think about trying to sit on a—"

He pried her hand off his pants. "Okay, okay. I get the picture. Get ready. Here comes another one. Deep breath now."

"Awwwwwwww," she wailed. "I need to push."

"Look at my shirt, Tess, and breathe like I'm doing."

"Don't tell me what to do," she snapped. "You didn't go to the classes. You're useless. I don't know why I took you back after you ran out on me, you sorry bastard. I don't need you to take care of too."

"That's the pain talking, sweetheart," he said, glad he had his phone conversation with Maddie.

"Don't sweetheart me, you jackass. It's not the pain. It's my brain finally coming to its senses about you. Why I thought you'd ever be daddy material, I'll never know."

Nick saw the nurse shrug and give him a half smile. He understood at an intellectual level that this was not Tess's most rational moment. But at an emotional one, he wondered why he had even considered staying with the woman who had neglected to tell him she was expecting his baby. Dumb luck had put them both in the same place at the same time. Otherwise, he would have never known he had fathered a child.

At that moment, he made the decision he had been waffling over for weeks. He would keep his cool during the remainder of her labor and delivery and hang around long enough for her to get home and settled. Then he was going to get the hell out of Dodge.

"Just pant and blow and rest between the contractions. It'll be over soon," he repeated before she let loose with another diatribe aimed directly at him. This one would have made a sailor blush.

Now he was really pissed. And in that moment he had to dig deep to stop himself from walking out of the labor room and letting Miss Independent have the baby all by her herself.

But while his sense of pride had been injured, his sense of obligation—or at least knowing what his mother would say if he walked away—kept him in the room.

He closed his eyes and cleared his brain of all negative thoughts.

"I can only imagine how this must feel, but you're doing a great job. It won't be too much longer until you're holding the baby— holding Michael—in your arms." It seemed odd to say the baby's name aloud, and he wasn't sure he'd ever even said it before.

His folks would be disappointed their grandson wouldn't carry their last name. At least Tess had promised to let them have contact with the baby, and he prayed her current foul mood didn't alter that promise.

She could make and break a million promises to him, but he couldn't bear the thought of his parents being hurt, especially after all they'd done to help make Tess's weeks of bed rest easier.

"Here comes another one," he warned. The monitor had proven to be invaluable for keeping on top of the contractions. "Look at my face and breathe with me."

With his encouragement and the nurse's, she rode the wave of half a dozen more contractions before the nurse checked Tess's dilation progress again.

"You're fully dilated, sweetie," Karen declared. "I'll notify the doctor. Then we'll get you propped up a little and with the next contraction you can start pushing."

"Oh, thank God." Tess's relief was evident in the tone of her voice.

"Is there anyone else you'd like in here for the baby's birth?" Karen asked after she'd texted the doctor. "We have room for a crowd."

Nick weighed the questioning gaze that passed between them.

"It's your call. My mom and dad are here and Maddie might be too." Nick would love for his parents to witness the birth, but he would never insist.

Tess took only seconds to communicate her answer. "No. No one else. I don't want to worry about anyone else but the baby, especially since he's early."

"Don't you worry about him," a male voice said from the doorway. Dr. Merrell entered, clad in fresh scrubs and accompanied by another nurse he introduced as Linda. Efficiently, he donned gloves and a mask and situated himself on a stool at the end of the birthing bed. "There's a NICU doctor on duty in the hospital and he's already been advised he'll be needed to evaluate the baby."

He folded the sheet back to clear the way for the baby's birth, then shifted his gaze to Karen. "Who's keeping track of the weight pool?"

Another contraction hit before Tess could comment, and with Nick on one side and Linda on the other, they counted to ten while she held her breath and pushed with all her might.

Once the contraction ended, she flopped back against the pillow. "Weight pool?" she asked breathlessly.

"Yeah," Nick explained. "We've all been betting on how much he's going to weigh. I've got ten bucks riding on five pounds even."

"I don't appreciate being wagered over, especially since gambling is illegal in this state." She exhaled a puff of air, trying to blow away a strand of hair stuck to her sweaty forehead.

Nick reached out and pushed the hair aside then laid a cold washcloth where it had been.

"Easy there, counselor," the doctor said as he laughed aloud. "The money goes to a group that knits blankets for babies in the NICU and older kids in the pediatric ICU. Surely you can turn a blind eye to our little fundraising effort."

The next contraction hit before she could reply. With support on both sides and Nick counting steadily in her ear, she pushed again and again until a squalling baby boy made his entrance into the world shortly after seven o'clock.

The doctor lifted him up and placed him on Tess's chest where a nurse covered him with a hospital baby blanket. His cries stopped as Tess stroked his tiny head.

"What was your hurry, Michael?" she whispered. "I could've waited a little longer for you." Tess continued to murmur to the newborn until the spell was broken by Dr. Merrell.

"Would you like to cut the umbilical cord?" he asked, holding out a pair of surgical scissors toward Nick.

Nick hesitated for moment, then grasped the scissors and cut the connection between mother and child.

"We need to check him out now," Linda said and whisked the baby away to be examined and bathed while the doctor finished tending to Tess. Nick resumed his position by the head of the bed. Tess lay quietly, eyes closed, exhaustion evident in her face.

Thirty minutes later the door whooshed open. "Here you go, Mama." A woman who had been introduced earlier as the neonatologist placed the baby in Tess's arms. "He's a bit of a lightweight, but otherwise he's fine. Barring any surprises, you should be able to go home in a few days."

He was swaddled in a white blanket trimmed with blue and pink, and a tiny knit cap covered his head. A few wisps of dark hair peeked from under the cap. Eyes as dark as coal blinked against the light and when the baby looked toward him, Nick gasped.

He was looking at a miniature version of himself.

Chapter Thirteen

Shortly after eight, the waiting room doors whooshed opened and Nick strode in. "He's here," he announced with an infectious grin curving his lips. "He was born about an hour ago and everyone's fine."

The obstetrics floor waiting room was filled with a large group anticipating the news. Maddie Worth and the entire Russo family were there.

"Please tell me you took a picture with your phone," Carol pleaded.

"Not one," Nick said and was greeted with jeers. "But I took a couple dozen and if the peanut gallery will stop booing, I'll show you." Nick pulled his cell phone out and revealed the pictures he had taken of Tess holding their newborn baby, his eyes closed and in one, his mouth stretched wide in a yawn.

He fielded questions from everyone at once. "They're still running a few tests, but he'll be moved to the nursery in a little while and you can see him there. It's down the hall and around the corner."

"Nursery? Why isn't he going to the room with Tess? Is something wrong?" Carol Russo's face was lined with grandmotherly concern.

Nick moved to his mother's side and wrapped his arm around her shoulders. "All the test results so far have been normal, and he weighs five pounds and two ounces. But because he arrived about a month early they want to place him under observation before letting him go to the room with Tess. And that'll give Tess a chance to get some sleep since she didn't get much last night." He rolled his shoulders and raised his arms above his head to stretch out the kinks. "Neither of us did."

Carol kissed Nick lightly on the cheek. "I know he'll be all right. I've been praying for him this whole time."

"Congrats, little brother. You did great." Bella stepped toward Nick and pulled him into a sisterly hug. "Does my nephew have a name?"

Nick licked his lips nervously. "His name is still under consideration. But I'll let you know as soon as he has one."

In turn, his father and other siblings congratulated him, and as his family exited the waiting room to make their way to the nursery, Nick pulled Bella aside. "Where's Lover Boy, by the way? I thought he'd be here with you."

Bella's mouth thinned to a straight line and Nick saw an almost imperceptible quiver in her bottom lip. "He…he's probably with his lover."

"He's with another woman?" Nick had met Ed Wallace on several occasions, and while he and the man had little in common, Ed had seemed like a nice enough guy.

Bella shook her head and Nick watched her blink back tears. It took Nick a few seconds to process what she meant. "He's with a man?" Nick's voice rose in volume.

"Hush," Bella commanded. She pulled a tissue from her pocket and dabbed at her face. "And yes, he's with another man. Please don't go all macho and threaten to beat him up. And don't mention it to the rest of the family yet either. I just found out three days ago and I haven't quite figured out how to tell them. They think he's at home sick with the flu right now."

Nick tried to process the news, but lack of sleep prevented all his synapses from firing in correct sequence. "I don't know what to say. What can I do to help?"

"Nothing right now." She gave a helpless shrug. "I don't even know what to do. But you have a new son and he's your priority at the moment. Come on," she said, taking Nick by the hand and herding him down the hallway. "Introduce me to my brand-new nephew."

When they reached the nursery, Nick found his family standing side by side in front of the window, all chattering at once about the baby that was front and center. He noticed Maddie standing to one side and approached her.

"Thanks for coming. I know it means a lot to Tess that you were here, and if you can stay a bit longer, I think she'd really like to see you."

"You've got a great big family here that takes precedence over me. Plus I know from experience that Tess needs to rest. I'll let her get home and have a couple days to settle in, and then I'll come to visit. I'll also offer unsolicited motherly advice." Amusement flickered in her eyes. "Give her a big hug from me."

"Are you sure you don't want to see her? I hate you came down here for nothing."

Maddie chuckled. "I think your mother was secretly relieved when she learned I'd gone to Lamaze class with Tess. So it wasn't for nothing. Tell Tess I'll see her soon."

Nick took her hands in his and gave them a gentle squeeze. "I will."

She shoved Nick toward the window. "Go. Be with your family and tell them all about labor and delivery."

The remainder of the day was a blur of phone calls and flowers. Between short visits from Ben and Carol and the constant monitoring and prodding by the nurses, Nick and Tess had little time alone. By dinnertime, Tess was situated in a private room and the newborn slept in a hospital bassinette at the side of her bed.

When the lactation nurse showed up to help Tess with breastfeeding, Nick wondered if he should stay or go. It wasn't as if he hadn't seen her bare breasts before. But feeding a baby—using her breasts for their intended purpose—seemed like such a private thing, and he excused himself from the room.

"Would you call Walter and let him know the baby is here?" Tess called just before he disappeared through the door. "Ask if maybe he can try to explain to Mama that she has a grandson?"

"Sure thing. I'll call him right now. I know he'll be excited to hear."

Nick dragged himself to the waiting room at the end of the hall and collapsed into a chair. He had been up for over eighteen hours and fully understood the meaning of sleep deprivation. After dropping six quarters into a vending machine and receiving a cup of bitter sludge in return, he made the call to Walter and listened as the elderly man promised to do his best to tell Pauline about the baby.

He ended the call and leaned back in the chair, stretching his legs out and rolling his head from side to side. What he wouldn't give for a good massage since his body felt as if it had been in a barroom brawl.

When his stomach growled and reminded him he hadn't eaten anything except the crackers and soda the nurse had brought him, he grasped the chair arms and pushed himself to a standing position. He wasn't excited about cafeteria food, but he didn't want to leave the hospital just yet.

Halfway to the cafeteria, his phone buzzed and Pete Clark's name appeared on the screen. Nick was tempted to let the call roll to voice mail, but he knew this was probably the announcement of who had won the photo assignment. And hadn't he vowed less than twelve hours earlier that he was going to take the job if it was offered? Hell, he was leaving town even if he didn't get the assignment. He'd make that trip to St. Kitts after all.

He tapped the phone to answer and lifted it to his ear. "Hey Pete. What's up?"

"You're up, that's what. Skill trumped nepotism and you, my friend, landed the job. You need to grab your passport, pack your best camera equipment and be in Sofia in two weeks."

"Yippee," he replied sardonically.

"Well if that's all the excitement you can muster, maybe—"

"Listen, Pete. I'm excited. I'm thrilled. I'm ecstatic."

Liar.

"It's just that I have a… I mean my… I've just had a lot going on lately with family and I'm exhausted at the moment."

"Nothing wrong with your parents, I hope." Pete had been to the Russo household on several occasions and Carol had treated him like visiting royalty.

"They're fine. It's just a little…well, I don't want to bore you with details. Can I call you back tomorrow when I've had a chance to sleep and handle some things?"

Pete agreed, and after he ended the call, Nick resumed his trek to the cafeteria and thought about the conversation. Why couldn't he tell his boss the truth?

My baby mama just gave birth to my son who looks just like me.

Oh, hell yes. That would sound just great—like a wannabe celebrity right out of the tabloids.

And exactly what *was* Tess to him? They weren't engaged. She had made it abundantly clear she wasn't interested in marriage just for the sake of legitimizing the baby's birth. Hell, she had made little effort to tell him she was pregnant.

Yet she was more than just a friend.

Yesterday he'd have considered an answer to Pete's offer a major decision he had to make. But after going through the labor and delivery process with Tess—a process he had heard most couples describe as bringing them closer together—the decision didn't seem so big anymore. His career meant everything to him, and this assignment would be an enormous boost to that career.

Tess had known all that his job entailed when they became involved. She knew about it when she got pregnant and decided not to let him know. She knew about it when he moved in to help her out after the doctor ordered her to rest. Why would she expect him to do anything other than take a plum assignment when it fell into his lap?

According to the doctors, barring any complications Tess and the baby would be released in several days. Nick could stall Pete, get Tess and the baby settled at home and then tell Tess he had to leave. His mother would help with the baby care now and soon Tess would have childcare arrangements in place. Plenty of mothers everywhere worked and managed just fine on their own. Tess would join their ranks and probably win a gold medal for her efforts.

There. Decision made. End of discussion.

Nick drove all thoughts of the subject from his mind and made quick work of an overcooked burger and soggy fries. He would love a beer chaser, but that would have to wait until he got back home. No, he would have his best Scotch. Neat. And enough of it to make him sleep straight through the night and halfway to noon.

*****

"He's beautiful," Maddie gushed as she cradled the six-day-old baby in her arms. "Holding a newborn almost makes me want to have another one and try for a boy."

"You're kidding, right?" Tess asked in disbelief. "I'm not sure I'd ever want to go through labor and delivery again. I sneezed yesterday and thought I would faint. Who knew the birth canal and your nose were connected?"

Maddie laughed. "You'll forget about all that the first time this sweet thing looks up at you and smiles." She brushed her finger gently down the baby's upturned nose. "Won't she, little guy? Huh?"

"I may forget about the discomfort, but I'm pretty sure my baby-making days are over. Right now I'm just trying to get as much sleep as possible and figure out how breastfeeding works. I feel like a cross between Elsie the Cow and Dolly Parton. I'm producing enough milk to feed triplets. And the advice I get." Tess sighed in frustration. "Everyone feels compelled to tell me how they couldn't produce enough milk or how I should give him cereal to make him sleep through the night or whatever else they think I have to know. I'm relieved Michael is healthy, and I just want to enjoy every moment of motherhood with my adorable, perfect son. But please tell me the advice stops at some time."

"I wish I could, but we mothers have a code we follow regarding advice. And I'm going to offer you the absolute best piece of advice I have."

Tess sent her friend a disbelieving look. "Not you too?"

"It's simple. Use common sense and ignore any advice that flies in the face of common sense."

The baby began to wriggle and turn his head toward Maddie's chest. "Sorry, pumpkin, but this isn't your feeding station."

Tess flinched at the mention of "pumpkin." "Here, let me have him. He's ready to eat. Again. I want to know who came up with the four-hour feeding schedule. If I tried to wait four hours to feed him, I'd be gushing milk and he'd be screaming his head off."

"Probably the same monk who's never seen a woman and also designed the hospital's sanitary napkins. They'd fit an elephant." Maddie stood and placed the squirming infant in his mother's arms. "Common sense, remember? And my other advice is to take every offer of help you get. Don't let pride stand in the way of some assistance with whatever they offer. And don't be afraid to ask for help. It's not a sign of weakness to admit you can't do everything."

Tess fumbled with the catch on her nursing bra and tried to arrange a receiving blanket over her shoulder while her hungry son began to whimper. She had been shy about nursing in front of anyone, but she didn't want modesty to cause her friend to leave. If she didn't get the baby feeding soon, the whimper would become a wail. She knew that all too well since she had heard it quite clearly in the middle of the night.

"Need any help?" Maddie offered.

Tess opened her mouth to refuse and then remembered her friend's advice. Maddie was still nursing her younger daughter. She knew what it was like to have a newborn. False modesty would serve no purpose now.

"Could you grab that pillow and put it under my elbow, please?"

Tess shifted against the pillow until she was comfortable, shrugged off the blanket and raised the hem of her oversized blouse.

She put the baby to her breast. He latched on quickly and fed with gusto, his tiny hand resting near her heart—the heart he had stolen when the nurse had placed him in her arms for the first time. Too bad he wasn't the only one who had stolen her heart. Life might be simpler without so many tugs at her heartstrings.

Damned hormones.

"There," Maddie said. "That wasn't so difficult, was it? And let Nick help you too. There are lots of things a father can do for a baby even if they can't feed them. And speaking of Nick, how are the two of you doing?"

"Would you mind getting me a glass of water?" Tess asked. "See? I'm getting the hang of asking for help."

Maddie's disapproving look wasn't lost on her, but the woman left the den and then returned with the requested drink.

"Any more requests to make so you can avoid talking about you and Nick?"

The common sense mentioned earlier should dictate telling her friend about the phone call she had overheard and the real possibility—no, make that probability—that Nick would be leaving soon. And even if he didn't have a career-making assignment in the works, she remembered the things she had said to him during labor and wouldn't blame him for taking them to heart and walking away.

"I've screwed things up, Maddie," she confessed, miserable over what had happened and what most likely *would* happen. Tess told her friend everything from overhearing the phone call to her outrageous statements six days before. "I have a new baby who wants to eat every two hours and Nick is probably leaving soon for Bulgaria. So that's how Nick and I are doing."

Chapter Fourteen

"I thought I saw your car drive in."

Nick turned and saw his mother standing in the doorway of the carriage house bedroom. She wore faded jeans and a turquoise sweater and had an apron tied around her waist. Great. Just great. He had hoped to avoid his mother until he had figured out how to tell her about his upcoming trip. In the course of his career with *Earth Events*, he had dealt with civil uprisings, natural disasters and manmade catastrophes. But his mother still had the power to make him feel like a wayward child.

Carol Russo wasn't going to be happy when she heard his news. Not happy at all.

"I've been making some casseroles for you. Things you can freeze and heat up when you need them," she said casually. He wasn't deceived. "How are Tess and the baby doing?"

"Fine," Nick replied in a clipped tone from inside the closet where he pulled two hard-sided camera cases from the top shelf. He stepped from the closet and dropped the cases onto the unmade bed beside an open suitcase. "They're both just fine." Turning on his heel, he moved back toward the closet.

"Wait just a minute, mister."

Nick recognized her no-nonsense tone. He'd heard it often enough during his childhood.

"What's all this?" She pointed to the items strewn across his bed.

Nick hesitated long enough to consider lying to his mother, then reconsidered. She deserved the truth. Hell, everyone deserved the truth, and it was time he came clean.

"I'm leaving on assignment to Eastern Europe in a week. I thought I'd get a head start on packing while Tess visited with her friend. The two of them will gab all afternoon and they didn't need me hanging around, getting in the way."

Carol opened her mouth to reply but no words came out. Nick had never seen his mother at a loss for words, but apparently there was a first time for everything. He had, however, seen the withering look she sent in his direction.

"Eastern Europe?" she asked. "If Pete Clark has to send you somewhere so soon after the baby's birth, can't he at least keep you in this country?"

"Pete doesn't know about the baby."

"And why the hell not? That's your child—your son. And you have a responsibility to him and his mother, dammit."

Nick rarely heard his mother curse. For her to use two profanities within seconds of each other made him want to turn tail and run.

Man up, buster.

"Pete doesn't know because, well…because I haven't told him."

"No shit."

Hell, dammit *and* shit.

"Pete only called about the possibility of the assignment last week, and then Tess went into labor early and life got crazy and I haven't had a chance to tell him about the baby."

"Have you told Tess about the assignment?"

Nick scrubbed a hand across his nape and stared at the stack of underwear and socks ready to go into his suitcase.

Carol released a loud sigh. "What are you planning to do? Sneak out in the middle of the night and leave a note on her kitchen table?"

He'd left a note the last time. It was part of the no-strings-attached arrangement they had. Only now there *were* strings attached, and they had a name   Michael.

"Are you really going to leave? Call me foolish and a hopeless romantic, but I actually thought you and Tess had something special. I thought the baby—your son—might make you want to settle down and stay here."

"Well Tess hasn't exactly asked me to stay. As a matter of fact, while she was in labor she made it pretty clear she could get along just fine without me. And I have to make a living so I can support my son."

"And you can't do that some other place besides Timbuktu and all those other places on the far side of the world where they keep sending you?"

"It doesn't matter if I'm in Timbuktu or Katmandu or downtown on Peachtree Street. She's made it perfectly clear how she feels."

His mother leveled her gaze at him. "But how do *you* feel?"

Nick swallowed hard and remained silent.

"That's what I thought," she said, wagging a finger at him. "You're in love with her and that baby, and you're just too damn stubborn to admit it."

He lifted his chin a notch. "I'm not saying I am, but if I was in love with her, it wouldn't matter because she doesn't love me. I grew up watching you and Pop, and never for a minute doubted you two loved each other. I don't want to be in a one-sided relationship, and I sure as hell don't want to be another of Tess's divorce statistics."

"Have you told Tess you love her? Have you two sat down and talked about your feelings for one another?"

Nick stared at the pile of underwear and socks again.

Carol shook her head in dismay. "Tell her, Nicky. Tell her how you feel and I think you just might be surprised by her response."

"She—"

"I need to get back to the kitchen," Carol interrupted. "Stop by the house before you leave and I'll give you the casseroles." With that, she turned and left.

Nick remained motionless as her steps sounded on the wooden staircase down to the drive. How had his mother figured out how he felt about Tess when he wasn't even willing to admit it? And how was he going to broach the subject with the woman who had basically told him to get lost?

Hell, dammit and shit, indeed.

*****

"Don't you think you should wait a while longer before you and the baby venture out?" Nick put the last of their lunch dishes in the dishwasher and returned to sit across from her at the kitchen table. "You've only been out of the hospital for a week."

"I want to see my mother, Nick. I need to see her. It's been almost two weeks since my last visit. I used to go every few days before I was put on lockdown."

"I just don't want you tiring yourself too much. You're still recovering from childbirth and—"

"Oh, don't give me that crap." She interrupted before he could carry his statement any further. He had no conceivable idea how tired she already was and what she would give for more than three hours of uninterrupted sleep. But she wasn't going to tell him that.

Not after practically screaming *I am woman, hear me roar* at him while she was in labor. She had to keep up the appearance of handling everything just fine until he left for the assignment she had overheard him talking about.

Once he was gone, she could loosen her grip on sanity and have a good cry. "Women in all those far-off places you've traveled to give birth to their babies in the fields and go right on working. If you won't take me, I'll drive myself."

Nick's mouth tightened with annoyance. "And I'm sure you will. Even if I hid the keys you'd probably figure out how to hotwire the car."

"I already called Waterford and they said Mama is having a good day. I can have Michael ready to go in a jiffy." She gave Nick a beseeching look. "He's just been fed and I'm already dressed. We won't stay long, but I have to see her and show her that she has a grandson."

Nick nodded his head in defeat. "I'll take you, but I have the final say on how long you stay. Do we have a deal?"

Tess started to argue but reconsidered. Nick was right. She didn't need to overtire herself or the baby. Her mother most likely wouldn't understand about the baby or remember the visit. This was more for her own sake than for her mother's. Not taking Michael to meet his grandmother was like admitting she had completely lost her mother to dementia, and Tess could never do that.

She reached to the portable bassinette next to the table and patted the swaddled baby's tummy. "Deal."

They arrived at the memory care facility a little after one o'clock. Tess cradled the baby in her arms while Nick gently guided her the short distance across the parking lot with a hand at her elbow. The attendant buzzed them in and eyed the trio.

"Would you like a wheelchair?"

Remembering Maddie's advice about accepting help, Tess nodded and thanked the woman for her assistance.

"I have two children myself, so I know what it's like with a baby. Looks like this one can't be very old either."

"Eleven days," Nick said.

"Six hours and a few odd minutes," Tess added.

The nurse chuckled at Nick's confused expression. "I hear ya, sister. It's hard to forget childbirth and the sleepless nights once they get here. But trust me, it won't be long until you two are ready to have the second one," she said as she stepped away to fetch the wheelchair.

When hell freezes over.

"Do you want me to go in with you?" Nick asked as they turned the last corner to the long hallway containing Pauline's room. "I mean, what are the chances she will mistake me for your father again?"

"Who knows? But maybe just to be on the safe side you should wait outside."

When they reached the room, Nick took the baby while Tess levered herself out of the wheelchair. They moved toward the door, which was halfway open and Tess peeked inside the room. Her mother was asleep, and Walter sat by the bed talking in a low, soft voice.

"I love you, Polly. I've loved you for a long time. I just hate you were hurt so bad before. It's too late now, but I wish I had tried a lot harder to convince you to marry me. You would still be in here, not knowing who I am half the time, but we could have had the years before your memory went bad."

Tess blinked back tears. The man's words were simple but heartfelt and sincere. Tess had always known how Walter felt. She should have encouraged her mother to give Walter a chance. Now, there was no chance for them as her mother retreated further into dementia.

She stepped back from the door and turned toward Nick. She held out her arms for the baby, who chose that moment to wake and make a fuss.

"Who's there? What's going on out there?" Pauline called out, her voice heavy from sleep.

A chair scraped against the tile floor and within seconds Walter swung open the door.

"Well look who's here. Polly, you have company." The elderly man stepped aside and waved them in.

Nick held back and shook his head. "I'll just stay out here. We don't want a repeat of the last visit."

Apprehension swept through Tess. "But you'll come in if I need you?"

He smiled. "Of course."

Tess entered the sunny room with her arms full of squirming, whimpering baby. By her calculations he shouldn't be hungry again, but her son didn't seem to understand math. She reached back and rooted around in the diaper bag slung over her shoulder to retrieve a pacifier, but her hand came up empty.

Don't be afraid to ask for help.

But what to do? As much as she loved her mother, given her weakened physical state, Tess was reluctant to ask her to hold the baby unassisted. And she wasn't sure if Walter would be comfortable with the infant in his arms. On the other hand, he might be far more comfortable holding the baby than fumbling among the diapers and nursing pads to find a pacifier.

"Here, let me," Walter offered, extending his arms. "It's been a long time since I held a little one like him. My grandchildren are all grown, but my first great-grandchild is on the way. I can use the practice."

Tess handed her son to Walter and found the pacifier. But Walter's firm hold and calming voice settled the baby, and he stared up at his new attendant with eyes wide open.

"Figures." Tess shrugged. "He and I are still trying to learn the same form of communication. But we'll get the hang of it."

Meanwhile Pauline had left her bed and stood beside Walter, gazing intently at the baby in his arms. "Whose baby is this? Did you get a babysitting job for tonight, Tessie?"

Tess closed her eyes, ready for another round of Guess That Delusion. She had explained everything. Several times, in fact. But recent events flitted out of her mother's memory like wisps of smoke from a candle.

"This is your grandson, Polly." Walter held the baby so his face was visible to the older woman. "This is Tessie's boy. Isn't he a handsome thing?"

"Well, for heaven's sake, it's hard to tell with him all wrapped up like yesterday's fish. Take his cap off and let me get a good look at him."

Walter placed the baby on the bed and Tess removed his sweater and hat, revealing his shock of dark hair.

"He certainly doesn't favor you," Pauline stated bluntly. "Where did he get all that dark hair? And where's your husband? Did he let you come out all by yourself with such a little one?"

Tess could hear the disapproval in her mother's voice, and the internal debate began about whether to ask Nick to come into the room.

"And what is this boy's name?" her mother ask before Tess could answer the previous question.

"Michael. His name is Michael."

Pauline clapped her hands with glee. "Named after my father. He would be so proud. And what about his middle name?"

Tess took a deep breath, hoping Nick was close enough to hear. "Nicholas. After his father."

She had been considering the name change for a few days and had come to the final decision on the drive to Waterford. The baby's birth certificate listed Michael Reece, but changing a name was a minor undertaking. And it wasn't likely her son had become attached to his middle name.

"Nicholas." Pauline tilted her head and Tess could tell she was trying to connect the name with something—anything—familiar. "Have I met him?"

Before Tess could answer, a voice sounded behind her.

"I'm Nicholas, but everyone calls me Nick."

Pauline gazed at him, confusion creasing her brow. Tess held her breath, praying her mother didn't accuse Nick of pretending to be someone he was not.

"I'm sure we met at your wedding," she said, her expression softening. "But I have problems with my memory sometimes, so excuse me for not remembering you."

Tess could almost hear a collective sigh of relief. She wouldn't try to explain that while Nick was the baby's father, he wasn't her husband. The effort would be pointless. She would just enjoy this moment, watching her mother make cooing noises at her grandson and count his tiny fingers.

And she would enjoy having Nick around until he left.

Again.

*****

Nick double-checked the last fastener on the car seat and then checked everything again. Each piece of baby equipment he had encountered thus far had presented its own set of tricks for successful operation. He had become used to those tricks, but then his hearing played a trick on him. Or had it?

Nicholas. After his father.

He had inquired early on about the baby's name, hoping against hope she would include something to connect him with his son. This was no trick. Adding his name to Michael's pleased him. His parents would be pleased too, but he knew they'd be happier if the baby carried the Russo surname. He would be too.

He had cared for her when she needed help. Made sure she followed the doctor's orders—at least as best he could with a woman as headstrong as Tess. Back rubs, foot massages, cooking and housework. They'd all been done out of genuine concern for her and the baby. Tess's refusal to give his son the Russo name frustrated him. And frustration was not something Nick tolerated well. He had always been solution-oriented, but this time, no solution presented itself.

Nick knew better than to push too hard about the name. Tess had made it abundantly clear on numerous occasions that she could and would manage just fine on her own. And never once had she mentioned listing him as the baby's father.

Nicholas. He would be happy with that. Tess apparently was. But would she still be happy when he broke the news about his latest assignment? His departure was only days away, and he had been too much of a chicken shit to let Tess know. He had found himself too wrapped up in fatherhood to break the spell with bad news.

Six weeks ago, he had been clueless. Now a living, breathing, crying, pooping baby bore his name, and he enjoyed it all, especially the early mornings when he would hear Michael's first whimpers. Nick would change his diaper and dress him in a clean sleeper, wiggling Michael's toes while reciting a nursery rhyme or singing a silly made-up song.

For those moments, Michael was *his* baby to love and nurture. Then once he placed his son in Tess's arms for feeding, the control shifted and Michael became hers once more.

He slid behind the wheel of the Range Rover, and beside him, Tess had already leaned back in the seat and closed her eyes. He had planned to bring up the topic of the baby's surname on the drive home while Tess was a captive audience. Mad as she might get with him, she would never fling herself from a moving vehicle and leave her child motherless. Eleven days had shown him just how attached Tess had become to her son.

Their son.

And those same eleven days had revealed Nick's attachment too.

The trip home was silent but for traffic noise, Tess's soft breathing and the occasional grunt and snort from the baby. Tess had nursed him before they left Waterford, so he was sated and sure to sleep for a while.

As Nick braked to a stop in the drive, he nudged Tess's arm gently. Her eyes fluttered open and she blinked until awareness of her surroundings set in.

"We're home," he whispered. "Go on upstairs and lie down. I'll bring the baby in and put him in his crib."

He unfastened the baby carrier from the base and brought it and the diaper bag to the passenger side of the car. Juggling it all as he helped Tess from the vehicle had him wondering how she would manage it alone.

They entered the house and climbed the stairs in silence. After settling Michael into his crib, he moved to Tess's room and found her stretched out on the bed, already changed into a pair of comfy pajamas. Fatigue clouded her face. The visit had exhausted her, as he had known it would. But Pauline had appeared to understand she had a grandson. And he had learned the baby had part of his name.

Those were victories in his book, and he would take all the victories tossed his way.

"Need anything?" he asked. He leaned against the door frame, unsure whether to venture into the room. He wanted to talk to Tess—needed to talk to her so he could explain about leaving. But perhaps this wasn't the best time. Maybe tomorrow—one day closer to departure. And departure was imminent since he hadn't told Pete anything to the contrary.

"I'm fine. I think I'll rest until Michael needs to eat again."

"Call me when he does and I'll get him for you. I'll be down the hall." He pointed toward the guest room.

An hour later Nick still sat in the nursery rocking chair, watching his son. He had his cell phone in his hand, with Pete's number pulled up and ready to dial. Twice he had pressed the call button and twice he had immediately ended the call.

Nick had never hesitated about an assignment before, especially not one that would further his career and put his byline on the magazine's pages.

He had also never had a child before. A son who bore his name—or at least part of it. He had been waffling about the assignment before the baby's birth and then decided to accept after Tess's tirade during her labor.

Now? Now he questioned whether he had taken that tirade too personally, given Tess had been under stress and in pain. He also understood why his dad boasted so about his children and grandchildren. Blood was thicker than water, but he couldn't bear the thought of thousands of miles of water separating him from this child. Would emailed photos and video clips be enough when he had just spent sixty minutes simply watching a baby sleep?

The Bulgaria assignment could be the gateway to the big leagues for him. It could provide him the professional respect he desired and a lifestyle many only dreamed of. And it could ensure his son never lacked for anything.

The baby's first hungry whimpers interrupted his daydream of taking Michael and Tess skiing in the Alps or to see koalas in Australia. Nick levered from the chair, scooped the baby from the crib and carried him to the changing table. His diaper-changing skills were still at the novice level, and the wiggling infant challenged them.

"Don't make me look bad, okay buddy? I don't want your mama to check you out and find a half-ass…uh, halfway-fastened diaper." The blasé way he cursed was one more thing to add to the list of things that had to change.

As if understanding his father's dilemma, the baby stilled and let Nick complete the task. The moment he fastened the last snap on the tiny blue-striped sleeper, Nick heard movement at the doorway. He lifted Michael and cradled him in his arms, ready to pass the hungry infant to his mother for feeding. He inhaled the fragrance of baby lotion. Who knew how intoxicating it could be when it came from your own flesh and blood?

"I thought I heard him, but then he got quiet. I figured I should check to make sure…" Tess's voice faded and her cheeks colored. "I sound just like one of those overprotective mothers, huh? Making sure he's still breathing."

"The books say it's normal. And if it makes you feel any better, I've done it too." Nick nodded toward the rocking chair. "Do you want to feed him here or in your room?"

"My room. I still feel a little more secure propped in the middle of the bed."

Nick followed her back to the bedroom and watched as she settled in. He placed Michael in her arms, and then turned to leave.

"You don't have to go," she said. "Unless you have something else you need to do," she added quickly.

Nick needed to call Pete and he had to come clean with Tess. He had put it off too long and the deadline loomed. Deadlines were of the utmost importance in the journalism game. Beating the competition to a story often made the difference between mediocre and great, and Nick had always aimed for great.

He had made his decision. He just hoped it was one he and his family could live with.

"Yeah, I need to make a phone call, but it won't take long. I'll go downstairs so I don't disturb you."

And before Tess could comment, he spun on his heel and headed for the stairs.

*****

"Your daddy is going to have to leave for a while, but he'll come back to see you." Tess drew in a deep breath then blew it out slowly. She had to remain calm for Michael's sake. Lifting her pajama top, she held him to her breast, and he rooted for a few moments before he found her nipple and fed greedily. Tess continued the pattern of slow breathing and soon felt the tingle as her milk began to flow. The baby settled into a steady rhythm punctuated by the occasional grunt as he nursed.

He was too young to understand now, but Tess wondered at what age he would grasp that he didn't have a daddy who came home every night like other children did. She could prepare him for it. She would read books or consult a child psychologist. Whatever she had to do, she would make sure Michael understood he was wanted and loved.

Her friend Maddie had set out on a course of single motherhood, which Tess had deemed the worst decision her friend had ever made.

Maddie's plan had changed because of circumstances, and now she and her sperm donor-turned-husband had two beautiful daughters. If Tess was honest with herself, they had a life she envied. She had everything they had: a good job and successful career, a child, a beautiful home in the suburbs. Well, almost everything. She had a man who was willing to support his child financially but wouldn't be around to see the first smile, the first steps, hear the first words he spoke.

Noting that the baby had slowed his suckling, she eased him away and lifted him to her shoulder. Patting his back gently, she whispered in the tiny infant's ear. "Don't you dare say Da-Da first. If you say Mama first I'll buy you a puppy."

Realizing how ridiculous she sounded trying to bribe an infant who only understood eating, sleeping and basic bodily functions, she chuckled.

"What's so funny?" Nick entered the room as Michael released a loud burp.

"Nothing really," she lied. "He just makes such funny faces." Tess shifted the baby to the other breast and struggled to readjust the supporting pillows. Nick was probably coming to break the news of his departure. Based on the call she had overheard several weeks earlier, he would have to leave in a few days.

"Let me help." Nick shoved his cell phone in his back pocket and slid pillows around. Once the baby began to nurse again, Nick stretched out on his back across the foot of the bed.

"Thanks." She hesitated a few moments then continued, hoping her voice didn't betray her tenuous grip on her emotions. "Did you make your phone call okay?"

Hours seemed to pass before he said anything.

"Yeah. I had to call Pete Clark at the magazine."

"Because you care more about that Nike camera than you do about your own son," she snapped, immediately wishing she could take back the words.

"It's a Nikon," he corrected. "Nike is a running shoe. And I do not care more about a camera than I do about him."

"Then what about leaving for Bulgaria?"

Nick jolted to a sitting position. "You knew?"

Tess nodded. "I overheard the night he called you."

"And you never said a word."

"I didn't want you to turn it down out of guilt over me and the baby."

"I didn't turn it down out of guilt."

It took a moment for his statement to register.

"You…you're not leaving?"

Nick shook his head. "So see? That Nike isn't more important than my son." He inched closer to her and reached to run the back of his fingers down her arm, a gesture that sent a shiver throughout her body. "Or you."

"But what about your job? Your career?"

Nick shrugged. "It'll work out. And I'm kind of tired of living out of a suitcase anyway. These last weeks here have made me remember how nice home life can be. And I want to thank you for something too."

"For what?"

"The name." Nick's tone softened. "I'm truly honored you would name him after me."

"Well, you *are* his father."

"And I want to be the absolute best father I can be, which brings me to another point. I was wondering if we might be able to make another change too."

"What would that be?"

Nick leaned in and pressed a soft kiss to her lips. "If you would agree to be my wife so we could change your name too." He kissed her again before moving back a few inches.

"Wow," Tess whispered.

"That's all? Just wow? Have I stunned the silver-tongued she-devil into silence?"

Tess would have argued with his assessment of her, but she wasn't sure her voice would hold out. Nick had not only told her he was staying, but he had proposed marriage as well.

Getting Nick to marry her had never factored into her plans, but eleven days of motherhood had shown her that two sets of hands far surpassed one set when it came to managing a baby and a house. When she went back to work, that extra set could be even more useful.

And while she had never wanted to admit it, she had fallen in love with Nick. If she was truly honest with herself, she had probably fallen for him before she got pregnant. But her stubborn pride and insistence on never becoming dependent on a man had kept her from acknowledging her feelings.

But did he love her or was he asking her to marry him out of obligation? For Michael?

"Can I think about it?" she asked, despite knowing in her heart what her answer would be since, in her heart, she knew he loved her. But she didn't need to make it too easy for him, did she? He deserved a little payback for not returning her calls and for keeping her in the dark about being asked to leave for an assignment.

"Just don't think too long. My mom's decided to take my suggestion and start a sewing business and she wants my apartment to house it. So if I'm not staying here, I have to find a new place to live because I'm not moving back into the house with my parents."

"You can stay here as long as you like while I think."

Nick scrunched his face into a fake pout. "But I'd have to stay in the bedroom down the hall. I'd much rather share a room with you." The pout changed to a devilish grin.

His grin had captivated her the first night they met. And it still had the same effect on her. She was tempted to jump him right there but for the nursing baby in her arms, not to mention the warning from the doctor not to engage in sexual activity until she returned for her follow-up visit.

The baby chose that moment to pull away and fuss, a sign she had learned to recognize as a gas bubble in his tummy. She lifted him to her shoulder again and rubbed her hand up and down his back. He grunted and gurgled near her ear.

"What's that you're saying, Michael?" she asked. "You think I should tell him what? Well, I don't know if he'll like that but if you insist."

"Very funny," Nick said. "I'll have my stuff packed and be out of your—"

"Guest room. He said he wants you out of the guest room and into his mommy's room because that's where mommies and daddies belong, especially after they get married."

Nick's brows went up. "He said all that, huh?"

Michael released a loud burp.

"I'll take that as a yes." The grin returned. "When can I move in? And what about our oral agreement?"

Tess slid from the bed and placed the baby in the bassinette. Her own wicked smile appeared as she neared Nick.

"Null and void. You can stop worrying about it and in a couple weeks we can do all the funny business we want. Right now I just want you to kiss me. I've finished thinking about it. The answer is yes."

His arm circled her waist as he whispered against her neck, "I love you, Tessie."

Epilogue

Nine-month-old Michael crawled to the edge of the colorful beach blanket, grabbed a handful of sand, and shoved it in his mouth before Nick could stop him.

"Honey, will you give me—"

Tess held out a cool bottle of water with her left hand, which sported a one-half carat diamond set in antique platinum filigree next to a thin platinum band. "You'd think he would learn."

Nick grappled with the squirming child and washed the sand out of his mouth—the third time in as many days. Nick snorted and put the cap back on the bottle, then handed his son a toy to hold his attention. "This child might look like me, but he definitely has your stubborn streak."

"Stubbornness isn't necessarily a bad trait. I'm glad I insisted Michael come with us. He is the reason we're together so he deserves a beach vacation too."

This wasn't just a vacation trip. Tess and Michael had accompanied Nick on a combination business and pleasure trip to St. Kitts, the island he'd been scheduled to visit before he had become Tess's keeper nearly a year earlier.

When Nick had phoned Pete Clark to decline the assignment in Bulgaria, he had explained that unless arrangements could be made to accommodate his new status as a father, he would go freelance, pick his own assignments and sell the photos to the highest bidder. Pete, desperate to keep his top photographer, had persuaded the top brass to give Nick more latitude with the assignments he accepted. They had also put him into a consulting position working with young photographers as well as promoting the magazine to journalism students.

Once Nick had photographed the sunken treasure discovered by an amateur group of divers, the trip became a belated if somewhat unconventional honeymoon for the couple. They hadn't been able to take walks on a moonlit beach or share quiet intimate dinners because their son had chosen to keep strange hours while away from home.

"Maybe I should take him to play in the surf again," Nick said. "He seemed to enjoy it the last time and I'm hoping I can wear him out so he'll go to bed early tonight and we can eat in peace."

"You're the one who turned down Bella's offer to keep him while we took a honeymoon trip."

"She has enough on her plate dealing with Ed's fight over the house and the fact he moved his partner in with him. Besides, she was scheduled to move to an apartment this week so she wouldn't have to face Ed and Naldo on a daily basis." Tess narrowed her eyes at him.

"Hey, I have no issue with the guy being gay. That's who he is. But he was dishonest, cheated, wasted my sister's precious time and broke her heart. He better hope I never meet him in a dark alley."

"Calm down and go play in the ocean. She has the best attorneys in town and Ed is toast."

"Thanks for helping arrange that." Nick leaned across the blanket and kissed his wife. "And are you sure you wouldn't have rather gone to Paris later for a honeymoon? Mom and Pop said they could have kept Michael next month. We could have tried for baby number two in the City of Lights."

"I'm absolutely sure about this trip. I can't imagine anything better than being on a beautiful Caribbean island with my two favorite guys."

Nick kissed her again, this time a little more deeply. "Maybe we can try to make a baby tonight." He waggled his eyebrows in an exaggerated manner.

"Too late," she said.

"Well, tomorrow night. During his nap."

"What I mean, sweetheart, is it's too late to try," she explained, placing emphasis on the last word.

His brows drew together and he looked at her with uncertainty until he understood her meaning. "You're…we're…?" A broad smile brightened his face.

"I suspected before we left, but I brought a couple tests with me and they were both positive this morning."

"I'm…speechless. Stunned. And happy," he added when he saw the beginnings of a frown on Tess's face. "Enormously happy. At least this time I'll be around to help during your entire pregnancy."

Tess chuckled. "If it's like the last time, you may be glad you missed it."

"Hormones?" he asked tentatively.

She shook her head. "Puking. Lots and lots of puking. So far though, I feel fine."

"Come on, buddy." Nick scooped his son from the blanket and together they headed for the clear, blue St. Kitts ocean water. "You're gonna be a big brother. And you and I both are going to be there for everything."

If anyone had asked Nick to picture this—life as a family man— a year ago, he'd have called them ten times a fool. But *his* family was a picture seared into Nick's mind forever.

ABOUT THE AUTHOR

In 2001, Marilyn discovered romance novels quite by accident, which led to a renewed interest in writing. She's had over forty stories published in the confessions and romance magazines and taught a class in how to effectively write for this genre. She is a member of Romance Writers of America and her local RWA chapter, Heart of Dixie Romance Writers. Her involvement on the local and national levels has combined to give her a great love of the romance genre and to develop friendships that span the globe.

In addition to reading and writing, Marilyn loves to knit simple things, cook in the Crockpot, and garden in a few pots on her patio. Her motto is "Have passport, will travel," and she recently added Ireland and Wales to the list of 32 states and 21 foreign countries she has visited.

A native of North Carolina, she came to Huntsville, Alabama, by way of Frankfurt, Germany. She has lived there longer than anywhere else and calls it home. After raising two great sons, she loves to dote on her two granddaughters. Somewhere amidst all the above, she fits in a day job as an administrative assistant for a boutique law firm.

Did you enjoy this book? Drop us a line and say so! We love to hear from readers, and so do our authors. To connect, visit www.boroughspublishinggroup.com online, send comments directly to info@boroughspublishinggroup.com, or friend us on Facebook and Twitter. And be sure to check back regularly for contests and new releases in your favorite subgenres of romance!

Are you an aspiring writer? Check out www.boroughspublishinggroup.com/submit and see if we can help you make your dreams come true.

www.ingramcontent.com/pod-product-compliance
Lightning Source LLC
Chambersburg PA
CBHW060811120626
46557CB00001B/177